Re:Apotheosis

Also by Robert B. Marks

The *Re:Apotheosis* series:

Re:Apotheosis
Re:Apotheosis – Aftermath
Re:Apotheosis – Metamorphosis (November 3, 2023)

The *Road of Legends* series:

The Traveller on the Road of Legends
Magus Draconum
War of Succession

The Eternity Quartet, with Ed Greenwood

Seizing the Torch
Of Wizards and Watchers
The Conjurer's Treason
Hunting the Future
The Confession of C. August Gaston
Foolish Ideas Involving a Volcano

Re:Apotheosis

Robert B. Marks

Legacy Books Press Fiction

Published by Legacy Books Press
RPO Princess, Box 21031
445 Princess Street
Kingston, Ontario, K7L 5P5
Canada

www.legacybookspress.com

This edition first published in 2022 by Legacy Books Press
2   1

Originally serialized on Tapas.io from May 27, 2022 to November 25,
2022.

Cover illustrated by Foxtail (www.deviantart.com/wilsanne07/gallery/)
Cover coloured by Dabdab (https://dabdab.carrd.co/)

Interior art by Foxtail

This book is typeset in a Times New Roman 11-point font.

Publisher's note: This book is a work of fiction. All people,
organizations, publications and places used have been fictionalized, and
any resemblances to real people, places, organizations, publications and
events are coincidental.

Library and Archives Canada Cataloguing in Publication

Title: Re:apotheosis / Robert B. Marks.
Names: Marks, Robert B., 1976- author.
Identifiers: Canadiana (print) 20220259003 | Canadiana (ebook)
        20220259038 | ISBN 9781927537718 (softcover) | ISBN
        9781927537725 (ebook)
Classification: LCC PS8626.A75417 R4 2022 | DDC C813/.6—dc23

To Rei Hiroe,
Whose creations and ideas got under my skin, into my brain, and took up permanent residence...and made me a better writer.

From left to right and up to down: Daiki Yamato, Jack Death, Captain Infinite, Princess Stellaria, Jenny Calhoun, The Destroyer, and Atria Silversword

Prologue – The Destroyer

"Does the hero have a name?"

From his dark tower in the wastelands, The Destroyer stared up at the stars and wondered what was there.

The people of his world called him a devil king, but he had the powers of a god. He had raised his tower in a day, using his magic to rip the stone out of the earth and weld it into shape. That, at least, he remembered doing.

His memory had a lot of gaps.

He could not, for example, remember where his army came from. It was vast, conquering one of the Four Continents in less than a year. The second of the Four Continents had fallen in half that time. It was only a matter of weeks before the third would fall, and then it would move on to the fourth. With each new conquest his army became bigger and stronger. As far as he could tell, this was good.

He just had no memory of having recruited or created it in the first place.

The Destroyer had a lot of time to think and reflect. He spent his days alone, sitting on his throne waiting for something to happen. Every few days, one of his generals would come in and report something. And then they would be gone, and he would be alone again.

As he sat on his throne in contemplation, he realized there were other strange gaps in his mind. He knew he had to conquer the world, but he had no idea what to do with it once he was done. His conquered territories were used for replenishing and growing his army, but otherwise he left them alone.

And then there were his generals. Only some of them had names. For a long time that didn't seem odd – after all, that was how it had always been. He didn't have a name either. Some people just had titles. But now, The Destroyer was starting to think that didn't make much sense. Why didn't all of them have names? Why didn't he?

One of his nameless generals entered and bowed. "The hero has killed General Bringer-of-Darkness," he reported.

The Destroyer rose from his throne. "He will pay for his insolence!" he roared. "Let it be known that anybody who kills the hero will be rewarded with ten times their weight in gold!"

The general bowed and left. The Destroyer blinked. Why had he been so angry? He hadn't even heard of General Bringer-of-Darkness before today. And aside from which, the hero hadn't done anything that would even slow down his forces yet. The conquest of the Third Continent was moving according to schedule.

Does the hero have a name? The thought was so jarring that The Destroyer didn't realize he had been holding his breath until he exhaled again.

That night, he returned to the top of the tower and

stared out at the stars. There were other worlds out there, he was certain of it. And he could travel to them – all it would take was a brief exercise of his power, and he would be launched into the void, infinitely faster than the light from the stars he was watching.

And then it caught his eye. Something bright streaked through the night sky, heading from one star to another. With a wave of his hand and an intonation, he brought his scrying power to bear on it. His eyes widened – it was a person, a woman, by the looks of it, doing precisely what he had just been contemplating. Whoever it was, she was far away – so far that it would have taken the light of her passage at least four years to reach him.

For the first time that he could remember, The Destroyer smiled. The conquest of the world could happen without him for a while – he couldn't even recall the last time he had issued a proper order to his armies. He would follow this explorer's example, leave this world and see what was in another one. And to start, he would see the world that she had journeyed to.

With a brief exercise of his power, The Destroyer left his world and streaked through the void. As the new world opened up in front of him, he wondered if he would want to conquer it too.

Chapter I – Princess Stellaria

"I don't know where I am, and I don't know what to do."

Adam Jacobs has a secret: he's going to marry a character from a video game. This is not what some would call an "otaku" thing, nor is she a "waifu" – she will be his wife, carry his name, and bear his children.

This sounds like a fantasy, but all of it is true. I know this because I am the one Adam Jacobs will marry. I am Princess Stellaria, Keeper of Lore, the Sixth Princess of the Kingdom of Arcaniana on the Continent of Blessed Adventure.

I was born into one of the cadet branches of the royal family. My early years were happy ones, spent playing with my cousins and some friends, all carefully chosen by my parents, on the grounds of the family manor. Being in one of the cadet branches, I was outside of the line of succession. As, like all of the royal family, I had an innate magical ability, I was thrust into magecraft, and began my education into the mystical arts at the age of 10. My future would be spent in a library deep in study as a sage or living rough in the field as an adventurer. There were no other options.

If you are not born into a world like mine, it can be difficult to understand what it is to have a role set out for you from the time of your birth, and to fulfill this role without question. But for the last twenty generations, that had been the way my family, and my world, worked. I entered into the Academy of Magecraft and Wizardry without bitterness or complaint. There I made some of the dearest friends of my life, who I will remember until the day I die.

My grades in arcane lore placed me at the top of my class, and I found myself on the road to becoming a sage. While I took pride in my success, it felt empty. I envied those who had ventured down the road of combat and support magic, and found myself spending most of my spare time with them, learning whatever they could teach me. When I graduated at the top of my class at the age of 16 and was given the honorific "Keeper of Lore" and a placement at the Great Archive, I felt empty inside.

For the first time in my life, I felt as though I wasn't doing what I was supposed to be doing. I knew, deep in my heart, that I should be in the field, blasting monsters into pieces, and helping to save my world.

When the Hero of Prophecy's party arrived at the archive to seek wisdom for their upcoming journey, I took my chance. I told the hero about my hopes and dreams, about how I had spent my time learning battle magic, and begged them to take me with them and prove my worth.

To my surprise and delight, they said "yes." I don't know how badly I scandalized the Great Archive or my family by quitting less than half a year after starting, but

I had no regrets. For the next three years, I was battling the forces of the Great Darkness at the side of the Hero of Prophecy. And then came that terrible day.

We were exploring a dungeon filled with wild magic. Much of what we encountered was familiar, but much of it wasn't. Strange devices adorned the walls, panels that looked like they had once had blinking lights but now long still and silent. The problem with wild magic is that it is, by nature, random. You never know how it will warp reality, and it will never do the exact same thing twice.

This is getting difficult. It's not easy to write about the moment where you were ripped from your world and thrown into a new one. What I remember was that as I took a step, the floor was no longer solid. I fell out of the world, and suddenly found myself in a new one.

The streets were made of a hard dark grey substance and filled with people in strange clothes, more than I had ever seen in one place before. The air was cold and smelled foul. Loud machines roared down the streets, travelling with such speed it seemed impossible to cross from one side to the other with any safety.

For the first time in my life, I was truly terrified. As a graduate of the Academy of Magecraft and Wizardry and a member of the Hero of Prophecy's party I was familiar with teleportation, but this wasn't it. Not remotely close. I was in a new place, and nothing in it made any sense.

I spent the first day huddled in an alley, keeping to the shadows, watching people pass and catching snippets of their conversations. I could speak the language, or so I thought, but so many of the words were new and strange. I tried to comfort myself with the thought that the Hero of Prophecy and my comrades in the party would be looking for me, but that didn't last long – I knew enough to know that the wild magic that had brought me here would not repeat and that there was no place in my world that was *anything like this. I was alone. There was no rescue coming.*

That night, I cried myself to sleep huddled into a corner. There was no heat – there was nothing within reach that I could use for a fire.

I spent the next day trying to figure out what I could do. I had to get out of my alleyway, but the street was still filled with those fast moving machines. There was also the problems of my clothes – they were lightweight, bright and colourful, revealing my midriff, and looked like nothing anybody else was wearing. I could not leave my alley without attracting attention, and I had no way of knowing if anybody would be friend or foe. And even if I did leave my alley, what could I do? There was no way that the coinage I carried would be accepted as money here, nor would I be able to exchange it. I was worse than a pauper – at least a pauper knew how things worked, and where they could go for charity or a meal.

I did not leave my alley that day.

That night I did not cry myself to sleep. I felt too hungry, too weak, and too numb. I just sat in my alley until my eyes closed on their own and I drifted off.

The morning of the third day, I knew it was probably my last. I hadn't had anything to eat or drink since I had arrived. I was so weak I could barely move. All I knew was that there was no hope, nobody coming to find and save me. I was going to die alone and unmarked in an alien world.

And then I saw somebody stop at the end of the alley and look at me. Our eyes met for a moment, and then I looked away. I heard his footsteps approach.

"Are you okay, miss?" he said.

I took a deep breath to collect myself, but it broke into a sob. A tear rolled down my cheek.

"Please help me," I said. "I don't know where I am,

and I don't know what to do."

He nodded. "Okay. Can you tell me who you are?"

"I'm Princess Stellaria, wizard of the Hero of Prophecy's party."

He blinked. "Wait, like the video game I was just playing? I mean, you look like her."

I broke down into tears. "I don't know what a video game is. I don't understand anything here. Can you please help me? I haven't eaten in days."

"I will, I will," he said. "But you're saying something pretty unbelievable. Can you prove it? Cast a magic spell, or something?"

I took a deep breath. He loomed over me, tall and clean-shaven with dark brown hair. The hunger had drained all of my resources, including my magical power. There was perhaps one spell I could cast, but I didn't know if I had enough left for it to go off. I held out my hand and closed my eyes, unable to bear to see whether it had worked or not and spoke the incantation.

There was a moment of silence, and then he said, "Okay, I believe you." I felt his hand take my own and he pulled me up. "My name's Adam," he said, taking off his coat and draping it over my shoulders. "Let's get you to the car and get some food into you."

I didn't know what a "car" was, but for the first time in days, I felt safe.

It's hard to describe what it is like to discover that you are a fictional character. Adam showed me the game I was from, Chronicles of Arcaniana, on my second day of staying at the apartment he was renting for his first year of university. He was a gentleman – he let me have the bed while he took the couch. But, that was little comfort as he loaded up a saved game and I watched an avatar of myself *splashed across the screen in dialogue.*

I lost track of all the thoughts that went through my head. I remember thinking that if my world wasn't real, than what was I? Was my absence even going to be noticed, or would another copy of me just take my place as the adventure continued? And what of my parents, or brother, or sister? Would they ever know how much I missed them, now that I could never return?

For a week, Adam tended to me with the patience of a saint. I know he couldn't understand what I was going through, but he understood enough to let me work my way through it. He even helped me clean up after I had used a spell in front of him to get a cup I wanted to look at off one of the high shelves, not realizing it was on a base with a couple of candlesticks. At the end of the week, I had made my decision: I would build a life in this new world, and I asked Adam for help. I think I already knew what his answer would be before he said it.

"Of course," he said.

What I did not realize was that the first step would be a trip to a cemetery. When we got there, he led me to section for children.

"It's a trick from an old spy novel," Jacob explained as we wound our way through the headstones, looking at dates. "If you're going to live in this world, you're going to need identification, a bank account, a social insurance number, and for all of that, you need a birth certificate. So, we need to find a child who died who would be your age now. Then, we'll use the obituaries to find the name of her parents, send in a request for a replacement birth certificate, and hope they don't look at it too closely."

He stopped at a small headstone. It looked worn and neglected. "How do you like the name Anne Marie Sorenson?"

"Will you still call me Stella?" I asked.

9

He smiled. "Whenever you want me to."

"Then Anne Marie Sorenson sounds great."

One application to the Ontario government and three weeks later, I officially became Anne Marie Sorenson of Kingston, Ontario. Everybody called me Stellaria or Stella – we passed it off as a nickname. But, as I held the birth certificate in my hands, I realized that taking the name of a dead child didn't feel right.

"We have to do something," I told Adam. "Something to help the family, to pay them back somehow."

"I understand how you feel," Adam said. "But first we'd have to find them, and then we'd risk them finding out why we're interested in their daughter in the first place. And that could go very badly."

I frowned. "Does caring for the last resting place of the dead matter to the people of this world?"

Adam smiled and nodded. "Very much so."

"Then I know what to do."

That weekend, we returned to the cemetery with flowers, and placed them on Anne Marie's grave. I touched her headstone and said, "Thank you for letting me use your name – I promise I will do honour to it and never disgrace it."

Every weekend until the day we left for Japan we returned to visit Anne Marie with flowers. We also paid for a replacement headstone.

My new identity established, we began the next step of my new life – an education. After all, there was no school that would recognize a degree from the Academy of Magecraft and Wizardry. We spent weeks preparing to take the Ontario High School Equivalency Certificate test, which for some reason Adam kept calling a "GED." With this, I could enter his university as a mature student.

As we prepared for the test, I kept thinking back to what I was. There were so many questions that I wanted to ask the people who had created me and my world. When I brought this up with Adam, his eyes became sad.

"They're in Japan," he said. "It's a long way away, and we can't afford to get there. And even if we did, there's almost no way they'd agree to meet with you. And then you'd have to prove who you are." He took a deep breath. "But, we'll get there somehow. We'll get you a meeting. I just don't know how."

My breath caught in my throat when he mentioned proving who I was. My powers were already fading as the weeks passed. By the end of my first year in this new world, they were gone. It felt as though somebody had removed one of my limbs. Even if I told somebody who I really was, I could never prove it again.

But by the end of my first year, two other things had happened: I passed the GED test and entered Queen's University as a student in the physics department, and Adam and I had fallen in love.

I don't know when it happened. All I know is that one day, we both knew that we would spend the rest of our lives together. I met his parents, and they approved of our match. Adam was an art history student, and the same skills and intellect that put me at the top of my class in the Academy of Magecraft and Wizardry allowed me to catch up so that we both graduated and entered graduate school together, Adam taking art history while I studied quantum physics.

The day of our graduation was also the happiest day of my life – that was the day Adam proposed to me.

All the while, we had been saving money for a trip to Japan, although we still lacked a plan for getting a meeting with the people who created me. It was the year before graduation that Adam discovered a Japanese convention held every October in Tokyo, which my creators always attended. We now had a date. We just *needed to learn Japanese, buy our tickets, and hop onto a plane. We would go at the beginning of our thesis years, six months before our planned wedding.*

We had no idea of what awaited us, what we would gain, and what we would lose.

You probably think that this story is nothing more than a fantasy. But I'm writing this all down because it isn't. This is not only my story, and Adam's story, but the story of all the creations who followed me. All of them – Atria Silversword, Captain Infinite, Jenny Calhoun, Jack Death, Daiki Yamato, Saline, The Destroyer – walked here in this world. Some were our friends. Some were our enemies. Some died. All of them lived, laughed, loved, and mourned.

All of us were here, among you. This is our story.

Chapter II – Atria Silversword

"I don't want to watch my best friend die again."

The first thing Adam noticed when they plopped down on the bed of their Tokyo hotel room, tired and jet-lagged, was the view. The Tokyo Sky Tree towered over the skyline, the edges of the snow cap of Mount Fuji almost luminescent as the sun set behind it. He could already imagine it as an oil painting.

Stella yawned and lay back beside him, her long red hair spilling over the mattress. Adam leaned over and gave her a kiss.

"So," he said. "Have you figured out what you're going to ask them when you see them?"

Stella shook her head.

"Well," he said, laying back beside her. "You've got three days left to figure it out."

"It's not easy," she said. "Even if I try to tell them who

I am, they'll never believe me. And after all this time, I'm not even sure what I want to know anymore."

Adam glanced at the television and laughed. "I only just realized – we're in the land of anime. We should watch some on TV."

Stella propped herself up with a grin, her green eyes glinting behind her glasses. "Oh yes, we should."

Adam grabbed the remote from the night stand and turned on the television. The hard rock beat of the introduction for *Eternal Chronicle of Hyperborea* filled the room. Stella snuggled into his side as the credits ended and the episode began. The show's heroine, Atria Silversword, was planning the defence of a cavernous power plant, her mech Volandpanzer standing near a wall. The power source, a glowing orb in the centre of the domed chamber, rested on a large pedestal.

"Right," Adam said, "this is the one with all that military terminology that keeps tripping us up. I'm only catching about half of what she's saying. You?"

"Not much better," Stella replied. On the screen, Atria pulled herself into the mech and got into an argument over the radio with her love interest.

"Oh yeah, they split up at the end of the last season," Stella said. "I had forgotten."

"I hate to say it, but we should just watch the simulcast with subtitles," Adam sighed. "I'd like to understand all the dialogue."

Stella nodded. "Okay." A mischievous look filled her eyes as he turned off the television. "You know, we've got an hour to kill before the simulcast, and it *is* a brand new bed we're on..."

Adam grinned and gave her a deep kiss. "How could I ever resist your highness?"

After their lovemaking, they cuddled together and brought up the episode simulcast on Adam's tablet. The

14

opening credits flashed onto the screen. The scene opened up onto the cavernous dome and the orb, and Atria Silversword giving directions.

"So, that meant 'field of fire'," Adam said.

Atria climbed into her mech. A crashing sounded behind her.

Stella blinked. "Was that in the show before?"

Atria turned her mech around, activating the rapid-fire cannons. "Identify yourself!" she demanded.

"Why aren't there any subtitles here?" Adam wondered.

Stella stiffened. "Something's wrong."

A hole was ripped out of the wall. Into the chamber stepped a tall figure, looking like a demon lord out of some bad *isekai* anime. The expression on his face betrayed nothing other than the curiosity of a sightseeing tourist.

"Identify yourself or I'll open fire!" Atria shouted.

The figure stepped up to the orb and smiled. "This will do," he said. No subtitles appeared on the screen. "*Zveit telekinesis*," the figure intoned. The orb lifted off its pedestal and took a position behind him.

Atria opened up with the rapid fire cannon. Tracers streaked towards the figure's chest. The high explosive shells exploded against an invisible barrier.

"That was impolite," the figure said, raising his hand toward the dome. "*Zveit telekinesis*."

The masonry of the dome formed itself into spikes and slammed down into Volandpanzer, impaling it to the floor. The escape hatch popped open. Gasping and battered, Atria crawled out. The figure gave her a curious look, and then turned away to leave.

"You can't take that!" Atria cried. "The city will be defenseless!" She drew the pistol from the holster on her hip and emptied the magazine at the figure. The rounds exploded against the figure's barrier.

The figure turned back to her. "Very impolite," he said, raising his hand again. "*Zveit telekinesis.*" Masonry broke away from the wall, fashioning itself into an impaling spike, pointed directly at Atria's chest.

Adam glanced away from the screen. Stella had his arm in a death grip. "Something's very wrong," she said.

When he looked back, Atria was scrambling away, the hovering spike turning to follow her, but there was nowhere left to go – the debris from the dome collapse had created a corner. She pressed her back into the corner...and disappeared through it. Out in the city, to the south of the hotel room, Adam heard what sounded like a sonic boom.

Stella bolted from his arms, pulling on her bra. "We have to go find her."

On the screen, the strange figure had also disappeared. The video on the tablet glitched and threw up an error code.

"It's dark out there," Adam said. "Wait, what do you mean 'find her'?"

Stella was onto her grey turtleneck and panties. "Atria," she said. "She fell into our world, just like I did. I'm certain of it. We need to find her, and fast."

Adam pulled on his underwear. "Okay, but it is dark out there. Wouldn't we be better off doing this tomorrow morning, when we've got daylight?"

Stella hugged him. "Adam, she's going to be disoriented and scared and alone, just like I was. We can't leave her like that. We are the only ones in this city who have any idea of what she's going through or how to help her. Please, do this with me."

Adam nodded. "Okay. Of course."

Once they were dressed, they hurried out of the hotel. The neon street lights threw an artificial tint onto the streets and buildings, reminding Adam of a digital art cityscape.

"It's a big city," Adam said. "Do you have a plan?"

"Basic search pattern," Stella said. "The same sort of thing we did back in Arcaniana. They may be rusty, but I've still got the skills."

It took an hour to find her. Adam spotted her first, leaning against the corner of a building in a side street, her short blond hair and form-fitting green uniform haggard, her dark blue eyes wild. "I think I found her," he said, pointing.

Atria drew her sword and pointed it at them. "Who are you?" she demanded in clipped Japanese. "Where am I? What happened to the sphere?"

Stella held up her hands. "We're friends," she replied in Japanese. "This is a city called Tokyo. You're in another world. It's hard to explain."

The dark bladed saber shook in Atria's hand. "Who are you?"

"I'm Princess Stellaria of the Royal House of Arcaniana, Keeper of Lore, support mage to the Hero of Prophecy. I'm like you – I fell out of my world into this one five years ago. This is my fiancé, Adam."

"Prove it," Atria spat.

"I'm sorry, I can't," Stella said. "My powers faded away a year after I got here."

Atria recoiled, her face close to tears.

Adam glanced at Stella. "Do we tell her?"

Stella took a deep breath. "Look, this is going to be hard to believe, but you're a character in a television series. We've watched it. We were watching it when we saw you fall out of your world. That's why we came to find you. We're here to help."

"And you can't prove any of it!" Atria cried.

"We can, but not here," Stella said. "From what I've seen in your show, you are an excellent judge of a person's character. What is your judgement of mine?"

Shaking, Atria lowered her sword. "I think you want to help me."

"If you come with us back to our hotel room, we'll get you some food and explain everything," Stella said. "We promise nothing untowards will happen to you. Will you come with us?"

Atria nodded.

"Can you walk?" Stella said. "You look injured."

Atria scabbarded her sword. "Give me a hand up, and I'll manage," she said. Stella took her by the hand and helped her up. They began to make their way back to the hotel.

"When we have time, you're going to need to teach me your language," Atria said.

"Why's that?" Stella asked.

"Because your pronunciation of mine is terrible," Atria said.

They came to the hotel and entered the foyer.

"People are looking at me," Atria said. A couple of people held up their phones and snapped pictures.

"They think you're a cosplayer," Adam stated. "Dressed up as...well...you."

"I don't think I like this world very much," Atria said as they waited for the elevator.

Stella squeezed Adam's hand. "I've found it has its benefits."

When they got to the room, Atria placed her sword and scabbard on the table, sat on the armchair and took a deep breath.

"I'm going to get room service," Adam said. "Is there anything you would like to eat?"

"I really don't care," Atria replied. She looked at Stella. "You said you'd explain."

As Adam called room service, Stella sat on the bed

and folded her hands in her lap. "We're both from worlds created as fiction by the people of this world. You're from a story called *Eternal Chronicle of Hyperborea*. I think it was a light novel before it was an anime. I'm from a video game called *Chronicles of Arcaniana*."

Adam winced as the person on the other end of the line switched to heavily accented English as soon he started trying to talk in Japanese.

"So I'm just a character in somebody's story," Atria said. "You can understand why I have trouble believing that."

Adam finished with the order. "I just got us rice balls and tea. That seemed simplest."

"We can show you," Stella said. "Adam, bring up the previous episode."

"Yeah, sure," Adam said, wiping his eyes. He tried to figure out how long it had been since they had slept, but he was too tired to do the math. He pulled up the third season premiere of *Eternal Chronicle of Hyperborea* on the tablet, pressed play, and handed to Atria. The opening credits started to run.

"It takes a couple of scenes for you to show up," Adam said, rubbing his eyes again.

Atria's eyes widened as she saw who was on the screen. "That's–" Then, as she appeared in the episode and started talking, Atria stiffened. "Okay, I believe you, please turn it off."

"There's actually a really great fight sequence in this one," Adam started. "Worth it just for the–"

Atria grabbed his wrist and squeezed, looking into his eyes. A tear rolled down her cheek. "Please. I don't want to watch my best friend die again."

Adam blinked and turned off the video. "I'm so sorry, I wasn't thinking."

"Apology accepted," Atria said. "I'm going to need a

minute."

There was a knock at the door. Adam answered. It was room service, with rice balls and tea. Adam took them and shared them out. As he watched, Atria chewed on hers mechanically, her face expressionless. Then she wiped another tear from her eye and took a deep breath.

"You two are foreigners here," she said. "You don't speak the language here, not well. Why are you here? It wasn't to come looking for me – you didn't know I'd appear until a few hours ago."

"I want to meet the people who created my world," Stella said. "They'll be at a convention here on the weekend."

"You won't be able to prove who you are," Atria said.

Stella smiled sadly. "I know. They'll think I'm just another fan."

"Are you okay with that?"

"I don't know."

"And how did you end up in this world, anyway?" Atria asked.

"I fell through the floor of a wild magic dungeon," Stella replied. Her shoulders slumped. "It just happened. My parents, my party, my friends from the Academy, none of them will ever know what happened to me."

Atria stood and put her hand on Stella's shoulder. "At least you have parents to miss you. I grew up in an orphanage, and not a very pleasant one." She took a deep breath. "You say you can meet your creator in this place? I want to meet mine. I want to know why my best friend had to die."

Adam rubbed his eyes. "Okay. I think it was a light novel first, so if we find the author, we should be able to contact him. Or her." He looked up the series on his tablet. "It looks like your series was written by Junichi Kaguyama. And he lives in Tokyo...and he has a website

20

with an email address."

"So we just need to convince him I'm really the person he created," Atria said.

"We could send him a photo," Stella suggested.

Adam shook his head. "He'd just think you're a cosplayer."

"He created everything in my world?" Atria asked.

"He should have, yes," Adam replied.

"I know what to do, then," Atria stated. "What character sets can your device use?"

It took a moment to set Atria up with the email program on the tablet. For a few minutes she sat composing in a language that Adam didn't recognize. Finally, Atria hit send.

"I wrote it in Old Hyperborean," she said. "If he created everything in my world, he should be able to read it."

Adam yawned. "I really need to sleep. If you two want to stay up and keep talking, go ahead, but please do it quietly." He lay down on the bed and closed his eyes. Even though he could still hear them talking, sleep came swiftly.

When he woke up in the morning, Stella and Atria were still talking. Atria leaned back in the chair with a smile on her face, the open tunic of her uniform exposing the white blouse underneath.

"They were all clumped together, perfect for a meteor strike spell," Stella was saying. "So I let them have it. And right as it came down, that's when I discovered they had a mage, and he had a reflecting shield."

Atria gasped. "So the meteor strike–"

Stella nodded. "Bounced right off. Directly towards the tower on the hill. And that's when we discovered that the tower wasn't empty."

"Who was in it?"

"A wizard," Stella grinned. "With a reflector spell."

"So the meteor strike..."

"Bounced right back again," Stella said. "Landed right where I'd aimed it in the first place. Of course, by then they were gone...and so were we."

Atria laughed. The sound brought a smile to Adam's face. He turned on his tablet to check email. It chimed. He opened the new mail.

Atria and Stella turned to look at him. "It's from Junichi Kaguyama," he said. "He says he can meet us this afternoon."

Chapter III – Junichi Kaguyama

"Would it help if I told you that your story has a happy ending?"

Atria, Stella, and Adam sat at a table in the foyer of the hotel. Atria took a deep breath to calm herself. Her creator was running late.

"You're sure there wasn't a photo of him somewhere?" Atria asked.

"I didn't see one," Adam replied. "But, I also hadn't slept in around twenty hours, so I could have definitely missed something."

Atria took a moment to look at her new friends. Stella looked tired but happy after staying up talking with her all night. Atria couldn't imagine what it must be like to be stranded in a strange land for years without people she could really talk to about it. Then Atria frowned. If she couldn't find a way to get home, she was going to be just as stranded too.

"You okay?" Stella asked with her terrible pronunciation.

"I don't know," Atria said. "This is not how I imagined my day would be when I woke up in my own world this morning."

"You think he'll recognize you?" Adam asked.

"I'm the only one wearing this uniform," Atria replied. "He'd better." She undid the top couple of buttons of her tunic. Somehow, the military decorum didn't seem quite so important anymore. At Adam's suggestion, she had left her sword and gun in the hotel room.

A couple of girls came over, asking to get a picture of Atria in her uniform. They weren't the first, and based on what Adam and Stella had told her about this "cosplay" culture, she didn't figure they would be the last. She stood up and let them take a couple of snapshots, and then sat down again.

"As soon as we're done this meeting, I want some civilian clothes," Atria said.

"I spotted a store just across the street," Stella said. "We have enough saved up for the trip to buy you an outfit."

Atria took Stella's hand and gave it a squeeze. "Thank you for coming and finding me."

Stella smiled. "It was three days before Adam found me. I couldn't let anybody else go through that."

"There are a couple of people looking at us," Adam said, pointing. A stocky Japanese man in his late forties in a blazer and button down shirt, accompanied by a young lady in a white blouse and pink dress, stood just inside the hotel lobby doors.

"They don't look like they just want a photo," Atria said as they started walking towards them. The three of them stood as the duo approached.

"Are you Junichi Kaguyama?" Atria asked.

24

"I am," the middle aged Japanese man said. "Are you the person who sent me that email?"

"I am," Atria replied. "My name is Major Atria Silversword. You created me and my world."

"This is Aiko Mitsubi," Kaguyama said. "She's my illustrator."

Mitsubi bowed. "It is a pleasure to meet you. You look just like my drawings of you."

Atria took a breath. "Thank you, I guess."

"Can we sit?" Kaguyama asked.

Atria nodded. Kaguyama and Mitsubi pulled a couple of chairs over to the table and sat down.

"The email you sent me is very impressive," Kaguyama said, "but I've met fans at conventions who could have written it. I'm going to need better proof that you are who you say you are."

Atria gritted her teeth. "No, we're not doing this. Just tell me why my best friend had to die."

Kaguyama fliched. Atria felt a flash of anger. "I've had a very bad week," she said. "First, my best friend died screaming defending a village against an attack. I watched him die. You know, creator, the one who I'd known since the orphanage, the one I lost my virginity to shortly after entering officer training, the one who was my first crush? That best friend."

Kaguyama and Mitsubi traded a startled look. Atria pressed on. "Then, the capital's outer defenses came under attack. And right in the middle of preparing to defend the power stations that handle those outer defenses, some strange new enemy I've never seen before with horns on his head and a stupid looking outfit walked through the wall, stole the power orb, left the entire capital defenseless, destroyed Volandpanzer using the *ceiling*, and nearly killed me. Then, I fell through a wall into this world, where I found out that my entire world was created by *you* to entertain people. So I really do not care about proving a damned thing to you. I just want to know why Abel had to die in front of me. Just tell me that!"

Kaguyama swallowed. "That information about your love affair with Abel isn't in any of the books yet – just your full character description, and Mitsubi's the only other person who I've shown that to. I can't believe it – you're real!"

"Very nice," Atria said through gritted teeth. "I don't care. Why did Abel have to die?"

"I'm sorry," Kaguyama said. "He died because that's what happens in your story."

Atria rolled her eyes and turned to Stella. "We're wasting our time here."

"Please wait!" Kaguyama cried. "Let me explain!"

Atria took a deep breath. "I'm listening."

Kaguyama leaned forward. "When a story comes to life, like yours did, the writer doesn't write the plot so much as discover it. Your story unfolded in my head, and I just wrote down what happened in an outline, and then fleshed out the scenes later. I don't know how else to describe it – characters make their own decisions and carry them out. Those decisions have consequences. Those consequences create the next part of the story. Sometimes I have to tweak it to keep it under control, but when you have a story as alive as yours, it's better to avoid doing that. I didn't make any changes to what Abel decided. He died because he was the sort of person who could never leave innocent people unprotected, no matter how small the village or how great the odds. I am sorry for your loss, please accept my sincerest condolences."

Atria put her head in her hands and wept. She felt Stella's hand on her shoulder.

"Is she going to be okay?" Atria heard Mitsubi ask.

"Going through this is hard," Stella replied. "It took

me a week to process it all when I went through it."

"So Atria is not the first," Mitsubi said. "If I may ask, which character are you?"

"I'm Princess Stellaria, but everybody calls me Stella. I'm from a game called *Chronicles of Arcaniana*."

"And you don't speak Japanese?" Kaguyama said. "At least, not very well. Forgive me for saying so, but your pronunciation is terrible."

"Language localization seems to matter," Stella said. "I don't claim to understand all of it. My fiancé and I spent a year learning Japanese before we came here."

Atria took a deep breath and collected herself. She wiped her cheeks. "Forgive me, creator," she said. "I misjudged you. I thought you were a heartless god playing games with the lives of everybody I know. I apologize. It hasn't been easy having faith lately."

"Would it help if I told you that your story has a happy ending?" Kaguyama asked.

Atria smiled thinly. "With events of late, that's a bit hard to believe."

"If you come to my home, I will show you the entire outline. I'll show you how your story ends."

Atria blinked. Had she heard the hint of a quiver in Kaguyama's voice when he said that?

"My friends need to come with," Atria said.

"It will be a bit of a tight fit in the car, but okay," Kaguyama said.

Kaguyama's apartment was smaller than Atria expected it would be. A simple single-bedroom unit overlooking a park, the walls were filled with bookcases and blow-ups of cover art, most of which had Atria's face on it. Atria decided to spend as little time looking at the walls as she could.

27

Kaguyama pulled a large binder off one of his bookshelves and handed it to her. "Here it is. Your entire story, from start to finish."

Atria sat down at Kaguyama's kitchen table and opened the binder.

"The anime is on volume 7," Kaguyama said. "I'm right now working on volume 10, and there are four more after that."

Behind her, Mitsubi was chatting up Stella and Adam.

"I'm a graduate student in quantum physics," Stella was saying. "My research area is the imprinting of information on particles."

"How long have you been here?" Mitsubi asked.

"Five years," Stella replied.

Atria glanced up from the page she was reading. "The attack on the capital was a feint?"

Kaguyama nodded. "The Paladin Legion was actually attacking the communication hubs down south. But, you and Prometheus figure that out and stop them."

Mitsubi tugged on Kaguyama's sleeve. "Are you sure she should know all of it?" she whispered. "There are a lot of spoilers."

"It will be fine," Atria heard Kaguyama whisper back. "It's not like she'll share them with the internet."

Atria reached the end of the binder and closed her eyes. "My story does have a happy ending," she sighed.

"I'll be writing your reconciliation scene with Prometheus in this volume," Kaguyama said. "You save your world and end the story at his side."

"Thank you," Atria said.

"And there won't be any more slip-ups in the schedule, I promise," Kaguyama added.

Atria blinked. "Okay. Again, thank you."

"But there's something I don't understand," Kaguyama started. "You said that one of the power orbs was stolen. I never wrote anything like that, and I consulted on the anime scripts as well. That's not supposed to happen."

"I think it was another character who had travelled between worlds," Stella cut in. "We watched it happen."

Kaguyama sat down and rubbed his forehead. "This is very hard to wrap my brain around."

"Try being in the middle of it," Atria said. "Regardless, we need to find this person and recover the orb."

Stella leaned on the wall, pressing against Adam. "That won't be easy," she said. "If he's moving into other created worlds, then he could be anywhere in world media."

"We have to try," Atria stated. "Created or not, Hyperborea is still my world. It's my home, and what I've spent the last ten years fighting to save. Without that power orb, the capital will be defenseless. My duty is to recover it."

Stella held up her hand. "That said, I have a theory. I don't think his person can travel directly from one created world to another. I think he has to come to this world first. And based on the fact that he invaded your world in the Japanese localization, I think he's basing himself here in Japan. So, we can find him. It just might take a while."

Atria smiled and looked up at Stella. "I'll need help. Will you help me? Will you all help me?"

"Our tourist visa is only good for another thirteen days," Stella said. "But as long as we're here, you can count on us."

Adam nodded. "I don't think I could look at myself in the mirror if we didn't help you."

"I'll help," Mitsubi said. "However I can."

"As will I," said Kaguyama. "Tomorrow is free, so we should be able to meet and strategize then."

29

Mitsubi stared at him. "No it's not – we have that meeting with the publisher and the production company tomorrow. We set aside the day for it."

"Right, sorry, I forgot," Kaguyama said. "I apologize. I got caught up in the moment. What about the day after tomorrow? Is that free?"

"That's Saturday," Mitsubi said. "It's free."

Adam glanced at Stella. "We'll miss the first day of the convention."

Stella sighed. "That's fine. This is more important. We'll do the convention another year if we have to."

"Atria, do you have anywhere to stay?" Mitsubi asked. "I live alone, and I could put you up if you want."

Atria shook her head. "Thank you for your kind offer, but I'd rather stay with my friends." She motioned at Stella and Adam. "Assuming they'll have me."

Stella and Adam glanced at each other. "We'll figure something out," Adam said. "Get you an adjacent hotel room or something."

"At least let us pay Atria's share of that," Kaguyama said. "Also, if there's anything you need, please let us know."

"Civilian clothes," Atria declared. "Too many people are trying to take pictures of me while I'm wearing this."

"I don't have anything that will fit you, but we can do some shopping," Mitsubi said. "I'm free today."

"That's what we planned to do after this anyway," Stella said.

As the discussion devolved into selecting clothing stores to visit Atria smiled. She had the beginnings of a plan, she had comrades, and her story would have a happy ending. So long as the thief who invaded her world didn't gather any allies, she would be able to figure out how to defeat him, recover the orb, and save the capital.

Chapter IV – Jenny Calhoun

"What's the point of saving the world if there's always something worse coming?"

Jenny Calhoun was surrounded by monsters, her best friend was dead on the pavement behind her in a puddle of her own blood, and she had a long blade in an underhand grip in each hand. In other words, she was in her element.

"She was like a sister to me," she told the throng of growling werewolves. "You shouldn't have killed her." Despite herself, a cruel smile curled across her face. "It's time to get stabby."

The werewolves attacked. The first four didn't stand a chance.

She sliced the belly of the first one open as she dodged. She cut the jugular of the second on her way into a roll, and drove one of her blades hilt-deep into the skull of the third as she came back up. The fourth growled at her. In response, she plunged her free blade into its jaw, pinning its mouth shut.

With a yank, she freed both blades and stared at the others. "So stabby," she said, taking a deep breath. Even with her supernatural strength, speed, and agility, there were too many of them. But even if her odds were slim, that didn't matter. She could feel the blood of her monster slayer ancestors pumping, her heart throbbing, and the adrenaline flowing. All of this she had experienced many times before. It was expected.

The weird looking Asian tourist, on the other hand, was new.

He strode into the alley without a care in the world, wearing a costume out of a bad low budget fantasy series. Horns sprouted out of his head. A glowing and humming orb hovered a few paces behind him.

The werewolves turned to stare at him. He gazed back with curiosity. They growled. He said something in what sounded to Jenny like Japanese, raised his hand and intoned, "Zveit telekinesis."

Jenny jumped as a chunk of masonry ripped out of the building on her left and slammed into the monsters, smearing them against the pavement. The tourist looked at the smear with curiosity, looked at her, and then gave her a friendly smile, saying something else in what was probably Japanese.

Jenny realized that her mouth was hanging open. She closed it and said, "Who...what are you?"

The tourist said something else she couldn't understand and smiled again, looking as though he was trying to appear reassuring.

"I'm sorry, I don't speak Japanese, or whatever language that is," she said.

The tourist frowned and approached. Jenny tensed, her hands squeezing the grips of her knives. But, as the tourist put his fingers on her forehead and face, she didn't strike.

Something held her back, although she couldn't put her finger on what it was. Her forehead tingled.

"What an interesting language," the tourist said in perfect English, stepping back. "Are you aware that many of your spellings are not phonetic?"

"I hadn't thought about it," Jenny said. "I guess so? Who are you? What's your name?"

The tourist frowned. "I don't have a name. In my old world I was known as The Destroyer, but that's a title, not a name."

Jenny's hands tightened on the hilts of her blades. "What are you?"

"I don't know," The Destroyer said, kneeling and poking at the gore. "In my old world I was a demon king. But now I'm not. What creatures were these?"

"They're called werewolves," Jenny said, shaking her head. "I'm sorry, but what do you mean 'now I'm not'?"

"In my old world I commanded an army," The Destroyer said. "I conquered continents. But I don't know why. It was just something I did. And then I left. Now I'm travelling."

"Wait, you conquered continents?"

The Destroyer stood and looked around. "I suppose my army did. I wasn't with them at the time. They took the First Continent, and then the Second Continent, and when I left they were conquering the Third Continent."

Jenny thought her brain was going to melt out of her ears. "Do those continents have names?"

"Of course they do. I just told you their names."

"Who names the place they live the 'First Continent'?"

"The people who live there do," he said. "Is that strange?"

Jenny blinked. "Very. Those aren't really names."

The Destroyer stepped out to the street corner and

motioned to a large building at the end of the block. The orb floated behind him. "What's that?"

"That's a high school," Jenny replied. "I went there before all this," she gestured around her, "happened."

"A 'high school'," The Destroyer said. "What's it for?"

"You really aren't from around here, are you?" Jenny said. "It's for educating people. Making them smarter, I guess."

The Destroyer smiled. "That's clever! An entire building just for making people smarter. I like that. Every world should have one."

"Don't take this the wrong way," Jenny said, "but you really don't seem like a demon king, or a conqueror. Except for the horns, I guess."

The Destroyer sat on a bench and looked thoughtful. "I suppose I don't. Back in my old world, I had an irresistible need to conquer. It took me ages to realize that I didn't know why. It didn't make me happy. It never seemed to make my generals happy." He frowned. "I suppose it didn't make anyone I conquered happy. And then I saw somebody travel between worlds one night, far away, and I decided to follow. And when I got to the new world she had led me to, I couldn't understand why I would want to conquer anything at all." He looked around. "So I just travel now. At least until I think of something else I want to do."

"What's with the orb?" Jenny asked.

"Oh, I took that from the second world I visited. There's this one world that's a hub – you have to go there first to visit any other world. It's very busy and interesting. But, there's a problem. As soon as you arrive, any power or magic you have starts to fade away. It's very slow, and it would take years for a higher being like myself to lose all of my power. The orb replenishes me. And, travelling between worlds takes more power than I thought it would."

"So you just took it from another world?" Jenny said.

"Of course," The Destroyer replied. "I needed it."

A vampire leapt out from the shadows. Before Jenny could react, The Destroyer stood and caught it in midair by the neck. He looked at it with curiosity.

"What is this?" he asked.

"It a vampire," Jenny said.

"'Vam-pire'," the Destroyer said, rolling the sounds around in his mouth. "What does it do?"

"It, um, bites you and sucks your blood. And turns people into vampires, I guess."

"That seems very impolite," The Destroyer said, squeezing his hand shut. The vampire's head popped off and crumbled to dust. The Destroyer knelt and poked at the pile of fallen dust. "And untidy. Are there many of these vampires and werewolves in your world?"

Jenny sat down on the bench. "Half of the town is overrun. I mean, my friend and I thought we had saved the town – and the world, for that matter – from this primal evil. But then this gateway to hell opened up, and all these monsters came pouring out. And they killed my friend."

"Do gateways to hell happen often in this world?" The Destroyer asked.

Jenny sighed. "There was a time that I didn't think so. And then I got to this school, and learned that I'm some sort of chosen monster slayer, from a long line of monster slayers. And the monsters started appearing, and I stopped them, because I'm the one who slays the monsters. I was able to save my friends, but not all of them, and that was fine – you can't save everybody, right? Winning in the end is what matters, right?"

The Destroyer nodded.

"But then, worse monsters showed up. And I stopped

them, and saved as many of my friends as I could, but I couldn't save all of them. But I won, and that was okay, right? And then this primal evil showed up, and would have destroyed the world, but I stopped him. But this time I was only able to save one friend. And then the gateway to hell opened up, and I couldn't save my last friend." Jenny's shoulders slumped. "And I know that I'll find a way to close the gate, just like I always do. And I guess I'll make new friends. But, I don't think it will ever end. I think that once I close this gate, something worse will happen, or some other, even bigger evil will appear. It always does."

"I don't think this world makes you happy, Jenny Calhoun," The Destroyer stated.

"I'm just so tired," Jenny said. "What's the point of saving the world if there's always something worse coming?"

"This doesn't seem like a pleasant world," The Destroyer said. "Too many monsters and too much unhappiness. I think I'd like to see another, happier one."

Jenny sighed. "Wouldn't that be nice. Just leave and go somewhere without all the monsters. I wish I could do that."

"You can come with," The Destroyer said. "I don't mind."

Jenny blinked. "Wait, you serious?"

The Destroyer nodded.

"I could just go with you, like that."

"Yes."

"And this hub world you mentioned, does it have monsters?"

"I haven't seen any."

Jenny took a deep breath. It was all she could do to not start crying. "Yes, yes please, take me with you." She startled. "Wait a minute, how did you know my name is

Jenny Calhoun?"

"You know your name is Jenny Calhoun," The Destroyer replied. "I learned it from you when I learned your language."

Jenny laughed. "We are so going to have a discussion about boundaries when we get out of here. So, how do we do this."

The Destroyer held out a hand. "You take my hand, and we go."

She took his hand. The world became a blinding light, and she felt her entire body stretch. And then the light faded and she was somewhere else.

Jenny let go of the Destroyer's hand and looked around. She was standing in a side street of a city at night, bustling under neon lights. Animated signs flashed Japanese characters.

"We're in Japan," she said. "My god, we're actually in Japan!"

"This city is called Tokyo," The Destroyer stated.

"And there are no monsters here," Jenny said. "No vampires, no werewolves, no demons?"

"You mean besides me?"

"You don't count!" Jenny laughed. "I'm safe – I'm actually safe! There's no world ending evil out to get me here! No vampires or monsters to kill my friends!" She grabbed The Destroyer and hugged him. "Thank you, thank you, thank you!"

"You're welcome," The Destroyer said.

Jenny let go and stepped out onto the sidewalk. Grinning, she took a deep breath. Then her eyes fell on the animated billboard, and her entire body stiffened. She could feel her heart pounding in her chest.

She pointed to the advertisement. "Tell me what that says," she said.

The Destroyer looked at the sign. "*Monster Slayer*

High School Girl Jenny Calhoun," he replied. "Tuesdays at 9:30 PM on Tokyo Television." He cocked his head. "It's a very good likeness."

Chapter V – Reality

"What am I supposed to do in a fight, scream at them?"

Stella held out her hand and concentrated. This time she would try the full incantation – no short cuts. "Powers of the universe, hear my prayer: grant me access to the laws of nature and summon dancing lights."

Nothing happened. She took a deep breath and lay back on the hotel room bed, wondering how Adam was doing at the front desk with trying to arrange a second room.

Atria looked over at her from the table. Her pistol was in pieces, and she cleaned a spring with an oily rag. She wore one of the new outfits Kaguyama and Mitsubi had bought for her, a light blue cotton shirt and black jeans. "No luck?" she said in accented English.

"I suppose it was too much to hope for," Stella said in Japanese. "My powers faded away four years ago. There wouldn't be anything left now." She grabbed a pillow and dropped it on her head. "I'm useless."

Atria shifted to cleaning the barrel. "You're not," she said. "Also, please say that in English. I need to practice my pronunciation."

Stella moaned. "I want to be able to practice my Japanese too, you know. Give me a turn."

"Your Japanese is painful to my ears," Atria said.

"How did you do that, anyway?" Stella demanded. "Learn this much English this fast? It took us a year to learn the Japanese we speak."

"I told you, I stayed up late last night watching English dubs with Japanese subtitles on that tablet Adam loaned me. And, I downloaded a Japanese/English dictionary and used it for reference."

"That's insane," Stella said in Japanese.

Atria chuckled. "That, at least, you pronounced properly."

"No, really, what's your secret?"

Atria put the clean and oiled barrel back on the table. "All officers of the Hyperborean Army are required to take mandatory intelligence training and learn at least three additional languages to speaking fluency prior to promotion to Captain. I think Kaguyama used English as a basis for East Dakkian. They're very similar in grammar, and a lot of the words have similar roots. So, it was more like learning a new dialect than a new language." She picked up the firing pin and began cleaning it. "I also took codebreaking as my intelligence course elective, so I have a bit of an extra advantage."

"The 'e' between the 'd' and 'b' in 'codebreaking' is silent," Stella said.

Atria nodded. "Ah, thank you."

Stella sighed. "At least I can help with pronunciation. Not much else I can do. What am I supposed to do in a fight, scream at them?"

"There's plenty of roles in combat that don't involve dropping explosive spells on people's heads," Atria stated. "Sometimes just having another set of eyeballs doing overwatch makes all the difference." Atria looked Stella in the eyes. "You are not useless. Stop saying that you are."

The door opened and Adam stepped in. "No luck with the extra room," he reported in Japanese. "The hotel is booked solid for the convention."

"That's no problem," Atria said in English. "I've spent enough time in barracks that sharing a hotel room won't be a problem. I'll just take the floor and you two take the bed. Also, please speak in English, I'm practicing pronunciation."

"You're more of a prodigy than my fiancee," Adam said.

Atria smiled. Then winced.

"Right, if you two need alone time, just let me know and I'll make myself scarce for a while," Atria said. "I'll go spend time with Mitsubi. She really wants to sketch me." She blinked. "That's going to be weird, actually. I'd be modelling myself for things in my own future."

"So, do you have a plan yet?" Adam asked.

Atria sighed. "No. I've got a mission goal, but that's not a plan. We have to find the thief who stole the orb and destroyed my mech, recover it from him, and then I have to take it back to my world...which we don't know how to reach. And we don't know his weaknesses. And they've probably replaced the orb by now anyway, rendering this entire exercise futile in the first place. You want to talk about useless, look at me. At least you two have a life here. I'm just passing time."

"What happens if he keeps that power source?" Stella asked.

"Probably very bad things for somebody," Atria said.

"Setting aside the fact that the thief wouldn't have stolen it unless he could use it, if it's damaged and loses containment...let's just say that there's a reason those generators are around five miles outside of the capital. Still, what the hell am I doing?" She shook her head and reassembled her gun, checking the chamber once it was complete before re-holstering it.

"Why did you do that?" Adam asked. "Checking if it's loaded right after putting it back together."

"It's just gun safety," Atria replied. "You always check the chamber to see if it's loaded whenever you pick up or put down a gun. No exceptions."

"Seems a bit excessive."

Atria held up one of the magazines. "These are explosive rounds. If one of these is fired accidentally, it would put a hole the size of your fist through the wall. You don't want to know what it would do to a person." She put down the gun and picked up her belt. "You said you lost your powers. That's magic, though – would it affect technology like my anti-gravity belt?"

"Depends," Stella said. "If the technology doesn't violate the physics of this world, it should be fine. If it does, then theoretically its effects would fade too."

"Right," Atria said. "We'll assume that the antigrav is only good for another twelve weeks then. Bullets shouldn't be affected."

Stella looked at Adam, who stared at them with a wistful look. Then he looked away. "Are you okay, sweetie?" she asked.

"I'm fine, don't worry about it. Just wondering if Kaguyama and Mitsubi are out of their meeting yet."

"Just let me know if you need something."

Atria chuckled. "He's feeling left out."

Stella blinked. "Oh?"

"We're creations, and he's not," Atria said. "He'll

never really understand what we've gone through." She turned to look at Adam. "And that's fine. I don't care if you don't understand what I've gone through, you're still my friend. Right now I'm more worried about not having a plan."

"I can try looking through the fantasy animes some more to see if we can find this guy," Adam said. "Maybe we'll get lucky and identify him. It will be a big job, though – they do a lot of genre blending in anime, so I might need to look at some of the sci-fi as well."

"Assuming he's not from a book or manga," Stella said. "That's a lot of content to sift through."

Stella's phone whistled. She picked it up and checked the messages. "It's a text from Mitsubi," she said. "She and Kaguyama have finished their meeting, and they're wondering if we want to meet them for dinner tonight."

"I'm just driving myself crazy here so yeah, let's go out," Atria said. "I'm in."

Stella looked at Adam. He nodded. "Don't have anything better to do. Besides, maybe we'll cover enough over dinner that we can finish up early tomorrow and get to the convention after all."

"I'll text her back and say yes, then," Stella said, tapping at her phone.

"We'll need help from Kaguyama and Mitsubi anyway," Adam said. "Maybe if we describe him, Mitsubi can do a sketch." Adam suddenly inhaled. "We need to find that orb."

"They've probably already replaced it," Atria stated. "The capital is safe. There's no urgency here, outside of my wanting to go home and needing something to do."

Adam shook his head. "I just realized: the technology fades away if it breaks the laws of physics, right?"

"Probably," Stella said.

"So what part of the orb breaks the laws of physics

more, the containment system or what it's containing?"

Atria went pale. "It's a 30 kiloton time bomb."

Stella took a deep breath. "And there's no telling where or when it could go off."

Chapter VI – Crisis

"Everything I did, everyone I saved, all the people I
cared about who I lost, it was all for nothing."

As Jenny Calhoun slept, monsters invaded her dreams.
First she watched, paralyzed, as they tore Troy, her
freshman boyfriend, to shreds. Then it was the turn of
Troy's friend Rachel, who they feasted on as she screamed
and screamed and screamed. Her parents were next. Then
they took her best friend. Jenny tried to call out, but no
sound came. The monsters turned towards her, but Jenny
was still paralyzed and her knives were gone.

She bolted upright to find The Destroyer close by,
watching her with concern. Sunlight streamed in through
the windows of the abandoned warehouse in which they
had taken shelter.

"You were in distress," The Destroyer said. "I did not
know what to do."

Jenny propped herself against the wall and wiped the tears from her eyes. "I was having nightmares," she said. When she saw the curious look on his face, she added, "Bad dreams. My friends dying. Not that any of them were real to begin with." She suppressed the urge to scream. "I'm not real, you're not real, they weren't real, our worlds aren't real. Everything I did, everyone I saved, all the people I cared about who I lost, it was all for nothing."

The Destroyer cocked his head. "You look real to me. I feel real to me."

"We were created by the people of this world for entertainment, Roy," she said. "They watched everything we did, everything we suffered, to pass the time. That's what we are."

"I am not known as Roy," The Destroyer stated. "I am known as The Destroyer."

"'The Destroyer' is the name of monster or a villain from a bad story," Jenny declared. "You're neither. I don't really know what you are, but you're not a monster and you're not evil. So I'm going to call you 'Roy'." She closed her eyes. "Besides, it's shorter."

The Destroyer looked at her for a moment. Then he said, "Is there anything I can do?"

Jenny smiled. "You're sweet, you know that? For now, just give me a hug when I need it, okay?" Her stomach grumbled. "I guess we should probably find some food as well. I think I've got about forty dollars on me – would they take American money in Japan? I can't imagine my credit card would be any good – the account doesn't actually exist."

"Why would you need money?" The Destroyer asked. "If we need food, I will just take some."

Jenny chuckled. "Right, 'higher being' and all that. We could absolutely rob a grocery store, and with our powers there's probably nothing they could do to stop us.

But, we need to keep a low profile for now." She glanced at the orb floating nearby. "And with that thing I don't think that's happening."

The anger rose again. She pushed it down. "Not that I'm all that opposed to robbing a store at this point. We've suffered a lot because of this world. Screw them."

"How have I suffered?" The Destroyer asked.

Jenny sighed. "You're still not getting it. We're fictional characters. We exist because somebody wrote everything about us down in a script or book or comic. You don't have a name because the person who created you never gave you one. You sat alone and bored in that tower of yours because they never gave you anything to do, or any reason to do it. Out here, right now, is the first time either of us have not had everything controlled by the people who created us. You have every right to be as angry about this as I am, and I'm amazed you're not."

The Destroyer blinked. After a moment, he said, "Do you need a hug?"

"Yes please," she said, and closed her eyes and tried not to cry as she felt his arms around her. "Nothing matters," she muttered. "Nothing I ever did matters."

After a couple of minutes she opened her eyes. "And if my world isn't real, and your world isn't real, then this must be the only one that is real," she said. "So we only need to worry about what we do here, in this world!"

The Destroyer let go and cocked his head.

"Don't you understand, Roy?" Jenny said. "We need money. But it doesn't need to be money from here – it just needs to be money that we can *use* here. We can get the money from any world. And since the only world that is real is this one, then it doesn't matter what we do in any of the others. We can just go to any world like this one and rob a bank!" She grinned. "Let's rob a bank! Can you bring us to a created world like this one?"

"I've never robbed a bank before," The Destroyer said. "Will robbing one make you happy?"

Jenny's smile faded. "I don't know. But I'm tired of being hungry and we need the money, so let's go and find out."

The Destroyer nodded. "Then I will take you to a world like this one. Also, what is a bank?"

If Jenny had to guess where this created world was set, she would go with New York City. But not a New York City connected to any reality she could imagine. For one thing, there seemed to be almost no women on the street. For another, everybody wore dark suits.

"What kind of story is this?" Jenny wondered.

The Destroyer gazed up at the tall buildings. "What are those buildings for?" he asked. "Are they banks?"

"They're office buildings," Jenny replied. "A bank would have some a sign saying it is a bank somewhere."

A hollow popping sounded from one of the alleys. Jenny tensed. It took a moment for her to realize why – it was gunfire. This must be an action movie.

"What is an office?" The Destroyer asked.

"It's a place where people go to work and earn money," Jenny said. "Let's try down this street – I think I see a sign."

"An office sounds very boring," the Destroyer said. "They should be high schools instead."

They walked down the street to a building with glass doors. A friendly green sign with a dollar symbol on it declared to the world that inside was the First National Bank. Jenny took a deep breath. This is all fiction, she reminded herself. Nothing in this world is real. Nothing they do here matters.

She opened the door and they stepped inside. A couple

of customers and several security guards stared at them, all wearing dark suits. A pair of tellers behind bulletproof glass also looked at them. They wore dark suits as well.

Jenny took another deep breath. "I can do this," she muttered. "They're all fictional. They're not real." Side by side, she and the Destroyer stepped up to the counter. Behind them, she could hear the orb humming as it hovered at a short distance.

The teller looked at each of them with confusion. Then he looked at each of them again. Then he asked, "Can I...help...you?"

"This is a robbery," Jenny said. "We'll take whatever cash is in the safe."

Beside her, The Destroyer smiled helpfully. "It's our first bank robbery. I am known as The Destroyer. This is Jenny Calhoun. What is your name?"

The teller shook his head in confusion. "This is a joke, right? Did Dave put you up to this?"

"You don't believe this is a robbery?" Jenny said.

"Well, you're not..."

"Not what?" Jenny demanded.

"...not wearing suits."

Jenny rubbed her temples. "Your objection to this being a robbery is that we're not wearing suits?"

"Well, all the bank robbers wear suits," the teller said. "It's how they hide their guns. And you've got no guns either."

"Are you seriously telling us that you're not going to believe we're robbing you unless we've got guns and are wearing suits?" Jenny said through gritted teeth.

"Well, at the very least we'd expect a blazer or sports jacket–" the teller started, but didn't finish. Jenny punched through the bullet-proof glass, shattering it, grabbed him by his shirt, and dragged him across the desk.

"Do you believe this is a robbery now?" she snarled.

Around her, she heard the security guards pull out their guns.

Beside her, the Destroyer's friendly look disappeared and became cold. "You would raise your hands against a superior being? That is very impolite." He raised his hand, and a spike of drywall and brick impaled one of guards, pinning him gasping to the wall. The others turned and opened fire on him, the bullets ricocheting off an invisible shield.

Jenny let go of the clerk and limbered up her shoulders. "Guess I'm getting stabby after all," she said, pulling out her knives. With a dash, she sliced open the nearest guard's side with one blade, and his throat with the other. Out of the corner of her eyes, she saw another guard aim his gun at her, panic in his eyes. He fired.

Her monster hunter blood throbbing in her veins, her blades flashed in front of her, knocking the bullets out of the air. "Nice try," she said, "but too slow." The guard died as he tried to reload, Jenny driving a knife into his temple up to the hilt. She looked to the Destroyer.

His arm was still raised, drywall and masonry ripping itself from the wall to impale the remaining guards. A couple twitched against the wall, blood spewing from their chests and mouths, before they were still.

From the corner of her eye, she saw the teller reach into his jacket and pull out a gun. With a flick of her right hand, her knife slammed into his forehead. She took a quick glance around – no threats left standing.

"That was easier than I thought it would be," she said, pulling her knife from the teller's forehead and wiping the blood off on his suit. She climbed over the desk and motioned for The Destroyer to follow her. "The vault should be back here."

They came to the vault door. The panel of a keypad flashed to the side of the reinforced steel door. "You can just rip that off its hinges, right?" Jenny asked.

The Destroyer poked at the door. "Yes." He motioned to the door, and an unseen force ripped it open, sending loose metal pieces scattering in its wake. Just inside the door was a large pile of money in neat bundles.

"Now we grab what we can carry," Jenny said, stuffing bundles of bills into her pockets. The Destroyer waved his arm, levitating a large stack. Jenny looked at the stack and nodded. "Right, let's go home." The Destroyer held out his hand. Jenny took it, and with a flash they were back at the warehouse.

"Did that make you happy?" The Destroyer asked, allowing the stack of bills to drop to the floor.

Jenny frowned. "Not really," she replied. "But, now we have enough money for whatever we need. Let's get some of this exchanged, and go get something to eat."

Chapter VII – Jack Death

"What kind of story is this?"

The assassins were coming for Jack Death again, but that was okay – by now he was used to it. The three in front of him would die just as all the others did.

His body moved with the speed that was the benefit of years of muscle memory. His aim with the Beretta 9mm was precise, every action flowing into the next: two shots to the chest of the first man to hold him in place, one to the head to finish him off. Grab his body and use it as a shield against the second. Two shots to hold the second man, one to the head. Throw the corpse at the third man to distract him, then two shots to the chest, one to the head. Stop and evaluate.

Seven seconds elapsed. Three targets neutralized. Nine rounds expended, six left in the magazine. No additional threats. Alleyway clear. One unexplained sonic boom.

Jack blinked. Sonic boom?

It had come from down the street, just out of sight. What followed was a pair of approaching voices speaking in English but making no sense.

The first was female. Young. Late teens to early twenties. "Do you have to say the name of the power each time you use it?"

The second was male. Adult. Light accent, possibly Japanese. "I don't know. That is how it has always been done."

"Try it without the words, Roy. I'll bet it will work."

Jack stepped back into the shadows to watch them pass. He blinked in disbelief as he saw them. The first voice belonged to a high school girl, 5'3", with long dark hair tied back in ponytail, wearing a purple t-shirt, ripped jeans, and long knives scabbarded at her hip. The second belonged to a tall Japanese man with horns on his head, 6'2", dressed like something out of a bad fantasy movie. Behind them floated a humming orb around the size of a beach ball.

Jack holstered his gun and began to follow them at a discreet distance. He was silent – years of training and practice as an assassin had rendered him undetectable whenever he needed to be. A ghost in a dark, bulletproof, three-piece suit.

"What kind of story is this?" the girl said.

The tall Japanese man looked around. "What are those buildings for? Are they banks?"

A movement out of the corner of Jack's eyes. Two more assassins after the bounty on his head. Jack moved into the next alley and drew his pistol, waited pressed against the wall at the corner where the alley met the street.

"They're office buildings," the female said. "A bank would have some a sign saying it is a bank somewhere."

The first man stepped past the corner. Jack moved.

53

Grab the first man by the arm, put two shots in his chest. One in the head to finish him. Pivot while holding the corpse as a shield. Two shots in the chest, one in the head. Evaluate. Three seconds elapsed. Two targets down. Alley clear. Magazine empty.

Jack ejected the magazine from his gun, reloaded it, and holstered it. Then he moved back onto the street. At an intersection, he saw the two strangers go into the First National Bank.

Jack hung back and watched.

He heard a flurry of gunfire and crashes. A couple of customers fled the building. And then there was silence. The strange pair did not emerge.

Jack waited another couple of minutes, and then approached the bank. He drew his pistol and opened the door. The carnage was unlike anything he had ever seen before. It took him a moment to get over the shock. *Remember your training*, he thought. *Assess. Evaluate.*

Seven targets down, six of whom were dead. Three killed by knife-work, one from a sliced throat with the expected arterial spray against the floor and wall, the other two from stab wounds to the head. Four targets pinned to the walls by spikes of drywall and masonry through the chest, three of whom were dead, one barely alive.

The survivor stared at him. Jack put a bullet through his head, putting him out of his misery. One bullet expended, fourteen left in the magazine. No sign of the pair responsible for whatever this was.

Jack climbed over the desk and shattered bulletproof glass shield. Debris from the vault door was scattered across the floor. The door had been ripped off its hinges and tossed to the side. Inside the vault was the remains of a pile of money. But there was still no sign of the strange pair. Somehow they had made their escape, but Jack couldn't even begin to guess how. He holstered his gun and stepped forward to take a closer look...

...and fell through the solid-looking floor.

There was a blinding light, and Jack felt his entire body stretch and snap back. And then he was somewhere else.

Jack shook his head to clear it. He was in a city, but it wasn't New York. Keeping to the side-street he had arrived in, he looked out and took stock. Most of the passers-by were Asian, speaking Japanese, and only a few of them were wearing suits. There were a few Americans or Europeans, speaking a smattering of different languages – tourists no doubt.

His training kicked in. First step: threat assessment, evaluation. Number of potential threats: zero.

Jack blinked. That couldn't be right. He reassessed.

Zero potential threats.

He shook his head. Forget that impossible number – he had to figure out where he was. He was obviously in Japan, and in a major city. The number of tourists was suggestive as well – probably a major hub, then. So, Tokyo, perhaps? There was a tower looming over the skyline that looked very suggestive. A snow-capped mountain to the west as well. Almost certainly Tokyo.

Still, there were zero potential threats. As impossible as that seemed, perhaps he should enjoy it. Jack wandered down the street, taking everything in. Turning a corner, he found a park with a smattering of families and tourists strolling through. A good, quiet place to take stock and think.

Jack found a bench with good tactical sight-lines and at least three routes for escape from the park, and sat down. Then he watched people pass by, enjoying the peace.

He heard the approaching man with ease, and assessed him through his peripheral vision. Male, early 30s, 5'6" tall. Japanese, well built, tattoos. Unarmed. Probably here to do an evaluation of his own.

The man sat down on the bench beside him. Jack didn't react.

"Not often that one gets to meet his American cousin," the man said in accented English.

"Yakuza?" Jack asked.

"You have a good eye," the man said.

"One needs it to be your American cousin," Jack stated.

"What is your name, cousin?"

"Jack Death."

"Are you associated with anybody?"

"Independent."

"Are you working, Death-*san*?"

Jack turned his head to look at the Yakuza. "No. And I'm not planning to."

"What brings you to Japan?"

"Just visiting," Jack said.

"And how are you enjoying your stay?"

"It's so still here," Jack said. "No tension in the air. It feels...peaceful. I'm not used to that."

"We pride ourselves on maintaining harmony in the face of visiting foreigners," the Yakuza said. "The guns laws here are strict, so I would suggest not being caught with those two pistols under your jacket. Otherwise, please enjoy yourself."

"You going to keep an eye on me while I'm here?"

The Yakuza shook his head. "No need. Your word is good enough."

"You're very trusting."

"No," the Yakuza said. "Just a good judge of character. You, I think, are not a man who would start a fight unless he was working. You are also a man with enough respect for his peers that you would not lie about whether you are working. That is good enough for me, and that means that it is good enough for us. Stay away from our interests and leave us alone, and we will leave you alone."

Jack nodded. "One last thing," he said, fishing out one of the silver tokens issued as underworld currency by the Great Council and handing it to the Yakuza. "Does this mean anything to you?"

The Yakuza inspected it and handed it back. "It does not, Death-*san*."

Jack bowed his head. "Thank you for your time and your answer."

"The honour was mine," the Yakuza said, standing and leaving.

Jack put the coin back in his pocket. It should have been recognized and useable as currency anywhere in the world. So, he was in Japan, probably Tokyo, but not his world's Tokyo. He'd need money. That would be easy enough, though – he could just pawn some of the tokens. They were silver, after all.

A commotion drew his attention. A mother and small child were making a scene near one of the trees. The child had just spilled her drink and was crying. Jack sighed. He knew what would come next – the child would be slapped and berated for her clumsiness. It was a common, universal little drama that everybody grew up with.

The mother knelt down and held her daughter, saying comforting words until the little girl stopped crying. Then, she gave the little girl a kiss and wiped the tears off her cheeks.

It took a moment for Jack to realize that his jaw was open in shock and close it. What the hell had he just seen?

There was something strange about this world, and he was going to get to the bottom of it, no matter what.

Chapter VIII – Luck

"I think I'm going to have to hate you for this, creator."

Stella munched on a rice ball and tried to put the convention she was missing out of her mind. Helping Atria was more important.

She glanced around the restaurant. A couple of tables had been put together so that the five of them could sit and talk while they had lunch. A television mounted to the wall was showing some slice of life program. If it had been later in the day, she imagined it would have been tuned to a sports game of some sort.

At Kaguyama and Mitsubi's insistence, last night's dinner had been a social gathering. Today's lunch was all about getting down to business.

"You foreigners are strange," Mitsubi said in Japanese, stabbing a french fry. "We take you to a pub so that you will feel more at home in our country, and you choose the most Japanese things on the menu."

Beside Stella, Adam chuckled. "We didn't come here to eat North American food."

At the end of the table, Atria had just finished explaining the situation to Kaguyama. Her hamburger lay half-eaten on her plate.

Kaguyama closed his eyes and took a deep breath. "I understand the urgency," he said. "I just wish I had something more helpful to offer. Without knowing the identity of this thief, we won't know what he can do. Even if we knew what he can do, without knowing where he is, we can't confront him and get the orb back. And if we do recover the orb, we still need a way to dispose of it without blowing up half the city."

"And the only one who knows how to travel between worlds on purpose is the thief," Atria added. "So, we either need to figure out how to do it ourselves, or convince him to help."

"And we can't go to anybody else," Kaguyama said. "They just won't believe us."

"Do you have a picture of him?" Mitsubi asked. "That would be the first step to figuring out who he is."

Adam shook his head. "I tried to rewatch the episode, but it isn't loading properly," he said. "There's some problem with the file."

"If we described him, could you sketch him?" Atria asked.

"I can try," Mitsubi said. "But that has problems of its own. If I've only got a verbal description to working from, there will almost certainly be mistakes in the drawing."

"I tried looking at all of the dark lord characters in the current season on AnimeWorld," Adam said. "Nothing matched."

"There's a lot that airs on TV here that doesn't make it to Western markets," Kaguyama said. "And that's assuming that he's not from some previous season."

"He didn't look like he was from a good show," Stella said. "His clothes looked like they were designed by somebody who just didn't care."

"So we're looking for somebody from a show or manga that is likely not very successful or well known," Mitsubi said. "That makes it harder, but not impossible."

Kaguyama glanced at Atria, and then at Stella. "I still don't understand how this is happening at all. And you've been here for five years? How long have characters been coming into the real world?"

Stella finished another rice ball. "I think it's been happening for a long time," she said. "I've got a theory, but it's a lot of complex quantum physics stuff that you wouldn't understand without having a background in it. The short version is that when enough people imagine a created world, the 'information' this imprints onto the particles escaping from their brain reaches a critical mass and creates that world as it is imagined. Under very rare circumstances, somebody like Atria or I can travel back along that pathway, arriving here."

"So why haven't we known about this before now?" Mitsubi asked.

"Why would you?" Stella replied. "Most of us probably don't last very long – this world is so alien that we just don't know how anything works. If Adam hadn't found me when he did, I would have died." She squeezed Adam's hand. "The ones who come from a story close enough to this world to survive the first few days probably figure out what's happening and just blend in. Besides, if you don't have some special power from your story, how would you ever prove that you are a fictional character and not some crazy person? And if you do have a power of some sort, it starts fading as soon as you get here, so after a few months you're just ordinary. Ordinary and lost." She

60

felt Adam squeeze her hand back. "Frankly, it's a miracle that we're sitting together having this discussion at all."

"We know that the thief can travel to created worlds at will," Atria said. "Perhaps there are others who can do that too who have already blended in." With a couple of bites, she finished off her hamburger.

"That assumes they haven't already gone back home," Stella said. "And it assumes that we can find them before their powers have faded, if we can find them at all."

"So we're left with trying to convince the thief to not just give back the orb, but to take it and me back to my world," Atria said. "That seems a big ask." Atria glanced at Kaguyama. "Something's bothering you – what is it?"

Kaguyama blinked. "How did you know?"

"You wrote me to be an expert at reading people," Atria replied.

Kaguyama hesitated and stared down at his plate. "What I told you about why Abel had to die, that wasn't the whole truth."

Atria stiffened.

"Everything I said was true. But, even so, his death, or the death of somebody like him, was necessary to the story to give it weight. Any character's journey is given meaning by the sacrifices and struggles that character has to make – how much they lose, or nearly lose. If it's not there, the ultimate victory feels cheap or unearned to the reader. That's just how storytelling works."

Atria took a deep breath. "So my best friend had to die so that whoever is reading or watching my story feels satisfied at the end?"

"I'm sorry," Kaguyama said. "There's no way to explain it that doesn't sound terrible."

"I think I'm going to have to hate you for this, creator," Atria said. "I know that's not all you're hiding, but I'll find that out later. I'm going to need time to get over this first."

"I understand," Kaguyama said. "I'm sorry."

"Please be kind to Kaguyama," Mitsubi said. "He just wants to tell a good story. We never knew that our characters could show up as real people or–"

Atria held up her hand. "Please stop talking. Nothing you say can make this better."

Adam glanced at Stella, looking like he was about to say something. Stella shook her head. Adam turned to watch the television.

"Does this television have a DVR?" Adam demanded. Stella blinked.

"It might," Kaguyama said. "Why?"

"I just saw him."

"What?" Atria demanded.

"He was in the background of the interview," Adam explained. "Excuse me," he called out to the bartender. "Could you rewind the show?"

The bartender shrugged and pulled out a remote. After a couple of seconds, Adam called out, "That's it - could you please pause?"

Stella rose to her feet. In the background of the interview was the thief who had invaded Atria's world, the orb hovering behind him. Beside her, she heard Mitsubi grab her notepad and start frantically sketching.

"That's him," Atria said. "Do you know who he is, creator?"

"I've never seen that character before," Kaguyama replied.

"Do you know where that place is on the television?"

Kaguyama nodded. "It's close – not far from an old industrial park. The park isn't used much anymore."

"Is this show live?" Adam asked.

"I think so," Kaguyama said. "I don't actually know."

"It's live," Mitsubi stated, still sketching. "We were

talking about it yesterday over lunch, remember?"

"I guess," Kaguyama said. "Sorry."

Stella looked over to Mitsubi to see her staring at Kaguyama with concern.

"This is our first piece of good news," Atria said. "I need to stop by the hotel room and grab my kit, and then we need to get to that industrial park."

"We can use our rental car," Stella said, glancing over to Kaguyama. "Once Mitsubi has finished sketching, you two go back to Kaguyama's place. We'll meet up there when it's done."

Beside her, Adam pulled out his wallet and dropped some yen on the table. "For our share of the bill," he said in Japanese. "I'm sorry if it's short. If it is, let me know, and I'll cover the rest next time we meet." He pulled up a map app on his phone. "Can you show me where this park is on here?"

As Adam got directions and Atria pulled on her double-breasted dark navy wool coat, Stella took a deep breath. For all she knew, she was about to go into combat with her fiancé at her side...and she was completely powerless.

Chapter IX – Confrontation

"Thank you for showing me the path to this world."

Atria took a deep breath as Adam drove towards the industrial park. Her green military tunic felt comforting and snug. Her sword lay across her hip as she sat in the car, her gun holstered and antigrav fully charged. She was as ready as she could be.

Her companions, on the other hand, were a different story.

"Adam, have you ever been in combat?" she asked in English.

"No," he replied, taking a right turn.

"Right," Atria began. "Here's what you need to know. If a fight starts, you're going to feel a burst of adrenaline. This will trigger your fight-or-flight response. Since you don't have any training or experience, you won't know what to do, and this will be paralyzing. This is normal.

You need to take measured deep breaths to slow down your heart rate – this will let you think clearly again. Once you're thinking clearly, follow Stella's lead and do exactly what she says."

"It's been five years since I was last in a battle, but I think I'll be able to handle myself," Stella added. "I'll keep you safe."

"And don't feel bad if you urinate or throw up," Atria said. "Those are normal too for your first time."

"So, do we have an actual plan here?" Stella asked.

"Find him and try to talk it out," Atria said. "Explain to him that the orb is dangerous, and ask him to return it. If that doesn't work, fight him into submission somehow. If things go bad, withdraw and try to figure something else out."

"And what do you want me to do?" Stella said.

"I want you and Adam on overwatch," Atria replied. "Adam, do you know what that means? It means I want you two hanging back and keeping an eye on the situation. If something happens that I can't see, I want you to shout a warning to me. Otherwise, don't engage unless there is no other option."

"We're here," Adam said, parking the car.

Atria took a deep breath, unbuckled her seatbelt, opened the door, and stepped out. She pulled her sword belt over her shoulder. Then she drew her pistol, checked the chamber, pulled the slide to load a round into it, and re-holstered it.

"So I guess we just walk around," Stella said, getting out and closing her car door.

"From what I saw on the map, he's got a long enough walk to get back here that we've got a reasonable chance of finding him," Adam stated. "If we're lucky, we'll catch him on his way back, or having just arrived."

"If we're lucky," Atria said. "Let's hope we're lucky."

Together, the three of them began to walk around the perimeter of the park, stopping whenever they reached an intersection to look down each street. Once they finished the perimeter, they started searching the interior streets. Occasionally somebody passed by, giving Atria a long look, but she ignored them. Let them think she's a cosplayer if they want.

"We've been here two hours," Stella said, "I think we missed him."

"How long do we have until sundown?" Atria asked.

Adam pulled out his phone and checked. "About an hour and a half."

"Let's give it another half hour and then call it a day," Atria said. "We can try again tomorrow if we have to."

Half an hour later, they began making their way back to the car.

"It was a longshot anyway," Stella said. "We had to get here before he did, intercept him on his route, and that was all assuming that this is where he's hiding in the first place."

They reached the car. Atria was drawing her gun to un-chamber the round when Adam called, "He's here."

Atria looked up. Standing in the middle of the street was the thief, still wearing those ridiculous looking clothes. She let the pistol slide back into its holster, raised her hands with palms open, and stepped forward.

"I'm just here to talk," she said in Japanese. "There are things you need to know."

"I recognize you," the thief said. "You were impolite and attacked me in another world."

"Which you attacked and stole from, and which I am sworn to protect," Atria said. "But as hard as it is, I'm going to let go of that for now. We need to talk."

The thief looked at Adam. "I don't know you." Then he looked at Stella. "I recognize you," he said to her.

"Greetings, fellow traveller. Thank you for showing me the path to this world."

Stella gasped. "You followed *me* here?"

"I saw your path across the heavens," the thief said. "I decided to follow. You have my gratitude – thank you for revealing all these new worlds to me."

Atria glanced at Stella. She was pale, steadying herself against the rental car. "This was all *my* fault?"

"Listen to me," Atria declared. "That orb needs to be returned to my world. It's dangerous."

"I am a higher being," the thief stated. "I have the powers of a god. There is no danger I cannot handle."

"You don't understand," Atria said. "It must go back!"

The thief raised his hand. A spike of masonry pulled itself from a nearby building. "You would tell a higher being what to do?"

Atria drew her sword and gun, firing twice on the spike. The explosive bullets shattered it into falling rubble. "I've seen that trick," she said, levelling the gun at his head. "If I have to beat you into submission and drag you back to my world, that is what I will do."

The thief began to rise into the air. "You will try, mortal."

"Gonna have to ask you to drop that gun there, lady," a new voice said in English. Atria looked to see a short American teenager is a purple shirt and ripped jeans. On each hip was a long knife. "See, that there's my guy Roy, and I can't let you go attacking him. So put the gun down and I won't have to get stabby."

"He attacked my world, probably killed dozens of people, and stole that power source," Atria said in English.

The teenager shrugged. "So what? Your world isn't real."

Atria trained the gun on her. "This gun is. Step aside."

The teenager drew both blades into reverse grips.

"Guess I'm getting stabby."

Atria pulled the trigger. The teenager's blades flashed, knocking the bullets out of the air. Then she charged. Atria barely had time to raise her sword to block the flashing blades before the teenager was upon her.

Stella stood by the car in shock. It was all because of her. Her fault. She looked at Atria. Whoever the teenager was, her blades flashed towards Atria with inhuman speed...and Atria's sword flashed back with equal speed. The teenager looked shocked for a moment, and then attacked again, Atria countering each blow. The thief hovered about forty feet above the ground, watching the duel with interest.

Stella looked down at her hands. If only she still had her powers, she could rain down magic destruction upon the thief, or freeze the teenager in place. But she didn't. Her magic was just a memory now.

Stella blinked. Her powers were long gone...but did the thief know that?

Atria crouched in a combat stance, her sabre before her in guard. The teenager was fast, but her movements were untrained and wild. Still, it was two knives against Atria's sword in close quarters combat – it was only a matter of time before the teenager got a strike in she couldn't parry. She needed a clear advantage.

"Nice sword," the teenager said. "You must be a main character somewhere. Anime, perhaps?"

"I'm Major Atria Silversword of the Hyperborean Army," Atria said. "I am here to recover my country's property. I have no quarrel with you – you can still stand down and let me do what I came here to do."

"That sounds like anime," the teenager said. "I *hate*

anime." She lunged in with a flurry of attacks, driving Atria backwards. Atria blocked and pushed the teenager away. With the hand holding her gun, she tapped the antigrav on her belt and jumped, propelling herself twenty feet into the air. She hovered, looking down at the teenager.

The teenager stared up at her with a predatory grin.

Atria took a deep breath, evaluating the situation. Firing directly at the teenager was pointless – she would just knock the bullets out of the air. However, all of Atria's rounds were high explosive, and asphalt would fragment nicely...

Atria trained her gun and fired, aiming for a semicircle around the teenager's feet. The teenager recoiled at the flying fragments and began running to get away from them. Atria empted the magazine, and then began to reload.

"Nice trick, anime girl!" the teenager called out, reaching the wall of a building and bracing one foot against it. "But it won't save you!" And then she launched herself at Atria.

Atria's eyes widened as the teenager cleared the distance between them and slammed into her, driving them both back into the wall of one of the buildings, the impact disrupting her antigrav. Together, they fell out of the air and hit the ground hard, the teenager using Atria to break her fall. Atria gasped, the wind knocked out of her, and felt the razor edge of one of the teenager's knives press against her jugular.

"I told you it wouldn't save you," the teenager said. "Goodbye, anime girl."

As Stella watched, the teenager pressed Atria back with a flurry of blows. With a push, Atria drove her back just long enough to hit a device on her belt and propel herself into the air. Then she opened fire, sending a hail of fragments flying around the teenager.

The thief took note and raised his hand. A spike of masonry ripped itself from a building wall, pointing towards Atria. Stella took a deep breath. If she was going to do it, it was now or never. She stepped forward.

"Enough!" Stella shouted at him in Japanese. "I am Princess Stellaria of the Royal House of Arcaniana, Keeper of Lore, combat wizard of the party of the Hero of Prophecy! You will stand down and return the orb at once, or face magical power beyond your imagination!"

The thief turned to look at her and cocked his head.

"I warned you," Stella snarled, holding out her hand and beginning to cast. "Powers of the universe, hear my prayer: grant me access to the laws of nature and all of its powers. Grant me the power of infinite destruction and the death of gods. Place the magic of all creation in my hands and bind it to my will–" The thief's expression didn't change, but the spike of masonry pivoted towards her. "–and I don't think he's buying it – run!"

She grabbed Adam and pulled him behind their rental car. The spike of masonry crashed through it, ripping open the cab, the tip stopping only an inch away from her nose. Then the car was ripped away from them and tossed aside by an unseen hand. The thief hovered before them, glaring. "That was very impolite," he said, raising his hand. A massive spike of masonry ripped itself from a wall, the wall collapsing into a heap of rubble, exposing the building interior. It trained itself directly at her.

Stella grabbed Adam's hand and squeezed. "I'm sorry, my wonderful love," she said. "I think I just got us killed."

The spike accelerated towards her. She closed her eyes.

And then her world exploded.

Chapter X – Superhero

"Throwing pieces of buildings at people is rather
impolite too, don't you think?"

Adam crouched behind the wrecked rental car, his
breathing ragged and eyes wide in disbelief. Everything
had gone wrong.

Atria lay still on the ground, the teenager holding a
knife to her throat. Stella's bluff had failed, and the thief
was hovering above them. A spike of masonry had
destroyed their rental car. And then the car was ripped
away by some magical power, slamming against the
wreckage of a building wall. A hovering spike of masonry
pointed directly at them.

He felt Stella squeeze his hand. "I'm sorry, my
wonderful love," she said. "I think I just got us killed."

The spike accelerated towards them. He raised his
hand and tried to cover Stella with his body. And then the
world exploded around him in a flash of silver and black

and a massive sonic boom.

Still covering Stella, Adam looked up. His eyes widened in shock. Floating above them, holding the spike in one hand, was a tall figure in silver tights and a black cape. He didn't need to see the man's face to know who he was – every boy anywhere comic books existed would know him. It was Captain Infinite, the Man of Titanium, the original superhero, the one who had defined and started the entire genre.

"Throwing pieces of buildings at people is rather impolite too, don't you think?" he said in fluent Japanese. With a squeeze of his hand, he crushed the spike into rubble. Then he turned to them.

"Do you prefer English or Japanese?" he asked in English.

"E-English," Adam stammered.

"Are you two alright?" he asked.

"Yes," Adam said. "But our friend–"

Captain Infinite glanced at Atria. "She seems to have regained her footing." Adam turned to look. Atria was indeed back on her feet, in a fighting stance with her sabre, facing off against the teenager, who kept looking at Captain Infinite in shock.

"Who are you?" Stella asked.

"I am Captain Infinite, but my friends call me 'Cap'," Captain Infinite replied. "I hope you will too. How about I take it from here?"

Stella nodded. "Okay," she said, her voice almost a whisper.

Captain Infinite turned to the thief and spoke in Japanese. "I couldn't help but overhear these fine people saying that you have something that doesn't belong to you. If you and your friend return it now, I'll let you both go. If you don't, I'll have no choice but to stop you."

"I don't take instructions from lower beings," the thief

72

declared. "Even those wearing silly costumes who can fly."

"You're one to talk about silly costumes and flying," Captain Infinite replied. "Last chance before I get serious. Give back what you've stolen."

The thief cocked his head and raised his hand. The side of a building exploded towards Captain Infinite, the pieces of masonry bouncing harmlessly off of him. "Well, I tried," Captain Infinite said. In a flash of silver, he slammed into the thief, driving him through the side of the opposite building.

Deep in the shadows, Jack Death watched the fight. His eyes widened as a literal superhero – *the* superhero – descended from the sky.

He frowned. If Captain Infinite had appeared, this didn't seem like a very fair fight at all.

Atria gasped, trying to regain her breath, as the teenager pressed the razor edge of her knife against her jugular. Her pistol had fallen out of her hand from the shock of hitting the building. She still had her sabre, but the teenager had her sword arm pinned, the sharp edge of a blade pressing against Atria's wrist.

"I told you it wouldn't save you," the teenager said. "Goodbye, anime girl." The pressure of the blade against Atria's jugular increased.

The world exploded in a flash of silver and a sonic boom. The shock wave washed against them, the teenager's blade jerking away from Atria's neck. The weight of her body still pressed against Atria's chest, but the pressure of the blade against the wrist of her sword arm was gone.

Atria blinked. The teenager was staring at something in the air, slack jawed. She turned her head to look. A man in silver tights and a black cape hovered between the thief and Stella and Adam, the rental car they had arrived in wrecked and smashed against the wall, a spike of masonry through the cab and engine compartment.

"Throwing pieces of buildings at people is rather impolite too, don't you think?" the man said to the thief. Atria looked again at the teenager. She was completely rapt. Atria pushed the teenager off her and rolled to the side, bracing herself against the wall as she rose to her feet. Every part of her body ached from the impact and the fall, and she was fairly certain she had cracked at least one rib.

Dealing with injuries would have to wait, though. Atria returned to a sabre fighting stance. The teenager got up slowly, eyes still on the floating man in silver. The floating man said something to Stella and Adam that Atria couldn't make out, and then turned to the thief.

"I couldn't help but overhear these fine people saying that you have something that doesn't belong to you," the man declared in Japanese. "If you and your friend return it now, I'll let you both go. If you don't, I'll have no choice but to stop you."

"I don't take instructions from lower beings," the thief stated. "Even those wearing silly costumes who can fly."

"You're one to talk about silly costumes and flying," the floating man in silver said. "Last chance before I get serious. Give back what you've stolen."

And then the side of the building opposite them exploded, chunks of masonry falling around them. Impossibly fast, the man in silver streaked into the thief, smashing both of them into the building on the other side. Atria blinked. The only person between her and the orb was now the teenager.

The teenager turned, shifting into a low combat stance, knives ready. Out of the corner of her eye, Atria saw Stella start to sneak towards the orb. The teenager glanced at Stella as well.

"Stella, don't!" Atria barked in English. "She'd kill you before you got halfway there – let me handle this!"

The teenager turned to face Atria. "Is she like us? A character from a story?"

Atria nodded. "We're the good guys, you can trust us. That orb is dangerous."

"Well then," the teenager said. "If she's fictional too, then when I'm done killing you, I'm going to kill her, just because you annoyed me."

"Not on my watch," Atria said, swinging into action.

Captain Infinite threw the thief through the wall of another building, following close behind. The thief shook his head and waved his hand. An invisible force grabbed Captain Infinite and slammed him into the ceiling, and then the floor. The floor collapsed beneath them, dropping them to the level below.

"I can keep this up all day, friend," Captain Infinite said, getting back to his feet. "Just give back what you stole and you can go on your way."

"You face one with all of the powers of a god," the thief declared. "Now learn what it is to be swatted by one." He waved his hand, and the invisible force threw Captain Infinite through the building wall, onto the street. Captain Infinite looked up, watching the side of the building collapse, the thief hovering unharmed above the wreckage. He launched himself at the thief, grabbing him and slamming him down into the debris.

Dust and falling debris clouded his eyesight. Captain Infinite glanced around. Somehow, the thief had gotten out from under him. Then the rest of the building fell on him.

He punched a hole out of the debris and flew up above it, taking stock. They were at least three streets away from where their fight had started. His hyper-hearing picked up the sound of a sabre clashing against long knives. The thief was nowhere to be seen below him.

So the thief must be above him.

Before Captain Infinite could check, the side of the opposite building exploded out towards him, showering him with massive chunks of masonry.

"That didn't work before," he declared, staring up at the thief hovering about thirty feet above him. "It won't work the next time either." He rose higher, far enough in the air to get a sense of the street layout. It was too even a match – he needed another approach.

Captain Infinite nodded. He knew what he would do. Accelerating past the speed of sound in an heartbeat, he smashed into the thief, sending him flying several blocks away. Then he headed back to the street where his new comrades still fought.

He landed to find the woman in the green uniform still fighting the teenager. The orb hovered a few feet away, unprotected. Captain Infinite approached and put his hand on it. So this must be what the thief stole.

A wave of nausea and weakness rippled through him. Captain Infinite blinked in shock. It couldn't be – the orb couldn't possibly be emitting *that* radiation, could it?

A chunk of debris struck him on the back of the head, sending him crashing against one of the few remaining standing walls. His vision swam before him.

Atria's blade struck with lightning speed, her body moving with all the benefit of years of close quarters armed combat training and experience. Every move she made, the teenager matched, counter striking with her other knife, forcing Atria into a back and forth that could only end one way if it continued.

The calculation was simple. She was injured. The teenager wasn't. She had advanced training. The teenager had unnatural speed and agility. But if she could just get one opening to exploit, she could end the fight. If she couldn't, it was only a matter of time before the teenager finished her off, and then Stella.

Atria gritted her teeth. Not on her watch. No more dear friends were going to die on her watch.

The blades flashed. The back and forth continued. Fatigue began to set in.

Behind the teenager, Atria saw the man in silver land by the orb. She smiled. Now it would be two against one.

It was just the distraction the teenager needed. She lunged in, slicing Atria's side under her sword arm. Atria staggered back, clutching the wound with her spare hand. Slick blood coated her fingers.

As she watched, the man in silver touched the orb and shuddered. A chunk of masonry flew from one of the piles of debris, striking him in the back of the head and smashing him against one of the remaining walls. The man in silver lay still. The thief descended from the sky, landing in front of the orb.

It was over.

"Please," she said to the teenager, "spare my friend. Kill me if you must, but let her live." The teenager looked unmoved and readied her knives for a killing blow.

"We have to leave," the thief said in English.

Out of the corner of her eye, she saw the man in silver shake his head and start rising to his feet.

"But I'm almost done here," the teenager said.

"The outcome of this battle is still in doubt," the thief said. He waved his hand, and the two of them floated away, followed by the orb.

Atria closed her eyes, leaned back and slid down the wall, taking several deep, ragged breaths. The blood remained slick on her hand as she clutched the wound. She heard a rush of footsteps. When she opened her eyes, both Stella and Adam were crouched over her.

"That's a lot of blood," Adam said in English, adding his hand to hers in applying pressure to the wound.

"I've had worse," Atria stated. "Has anybody seen my gun? I dropped it when I hit that wall."

Stella looked around. "I think it's buried under the rubble. Sorry."

The man in silver stepped over. "That's a pretty bad wound. I can cauterize it, if you want."

Atria looked up at him. "You have a first aid kit?"

"Laser eyes, actually," the man said. "Long story. It will hurt, but I can close that up."

Atria nodded. "Please do."

"I need a close look at the wound," he said, gently moving her and Adam's hands aside. "You need to hold very still." She felt the blood flow more freely. Then there was a searing pain. She closed her eyes and gritted her teeth.

"It's done," the man said.

Atria opened her eyes and nodded. "Thank you, and thank you for all the other help too, whatever your name is."

The man held out his hand. "I'm Captain Infinite. I guess you could say I'm a 'superhero'. You can call me 'Cap'."

"You're supposed to shake it," Adam whispered in her ear.

Atria shook Captain Infinite's hand. "A pleasure to meet you, Cap. I'm Major Atria Silversword. Those are my friends Stella and Adam. They're engaged."

"That orb you're trying to recover," Cap said, "what is it?"

"It's a power source from my world," Atria said. "The tall fellow in the silly clothes stole it. We're trying to get it back to my world before the containment fails, and it explodes."

"So, I've got some bad news, then," Cap said. "I got hit by radiation from that thing when I touched it. I think the containment is already starting to fail."

Atria sighed. "Lovely. We need to get back to Kaguyama's and regroup. I think we can call this engagement a complete failure. Where's the car?"

"What's left of it is over here," Adam said, pointing. "And part of it seems to be over there."

"So we're walking then," Atria said, scabbarding her sword. "Somebody help me up."

Cap held out his hand. Atria took it and stood up. Her head swam for a moment. "You look like you need more help," he said.

"Give me a moment," Atria said. "Do you know what is going on, how you got here, and all that?"

"I know this isn't my world," Cap said. "And that you're trying to recover that orb from somebody who stole it. Otherwise, I'm still figuring everything else out."

"The short version is that Stella, you, me, that tall person, and the teenager with the knives are all fictional characters," Atria said. "This is the world of the people who created us. Stella can fill you in on all the rest."

Cap blinked. "I'm not sure how to take that, or whether to believe it."

"We can prove it later," Stella said. "In the meantime, we should start getting back. It's a long walk."

They started walking, Atria leaning against Stella as they went. "Does anybody know who that teenager was?" Atria asked.

"I think she's Jenny Calhoun," Adam replied. "We watched her show back in Canada. She's a high school girl who fights monsters and saves the world."

"She's a hero?" Atria said. "That's one pretty unhinged hero."

"I take it you don't know who the tall fellow was," Cap stated.

"We've been trying to figure that one out for days," Adam said. "How did you get here, anyway?"

"I saw that tall fellow poking around in my world, followed by that orb," Cap replied.

"What did he steal from your world?" Atria asked.

Cap shrugged. "As far as I can tell, nothing. He just seemed to be looking around the city, dressed like some sort of shabby supervillain. And then he just disappeared. It was odd – no signs of teleportation or anything of the sort. I spent the better part of a day looking around the streets to see if he had just ducked into a building or alley, but nothing. Then I landed, and fell right through the ground into this world."

"Ah," Atria said. "For me it was a wall."

"Floor for me," Stella added. They turned a corner.

"So, there was a flash of light, and then everything was strange. It was New York, but not *my* New York. The skyscrapers were different. I flew down to my cabin by the lake about fifty miles out of the city, but it wasn't there – and neither was the lake."

"Wait," Adam said. "You commute?"

Cap nodded. "Beats apartment living."

"Right, sorry," Adam said. "Please continue."

"Then I flew to this tower in Antarctica I built back when I first got here in the mid-'30s. But it wasn't there, and neither were any of the landmarks around it. After that, I didn't know what to do. So, I just started flying. I was close to Japan when I started hearing your confrontation with that tall fellow and decided to check it out. You know the rest."

"Well, thank you for your help," Atria said. "If you hadn't arrived when you did, I think that Jenny girl would have killed us."

"It was my pleasure," Cap said.

"So, we need to get back to Kaguyama's and figure out a new plan," Atria said. "First, though, I think I want to stop by the hotel and grab my street clothes. I think my uniform is done for."

"If you've got a place to stay, have you got room for one more?" Cap asked. "I don't have anywhere to go at the moment."

"All of that is going to have to wait," Adam said as they turned another corner, motioning. A line of soldiers with combat rifles at the ready blocked the street before them.

"They're Japanese Self-Defence Force," Cap said. "I worked with these guys back in the '80s."

One of the soldiers stepped forward. "I must ask you to come with us," he said in heavily accented English.

Atria closed her eyes and took a deep breath. "Guys, I don't have any fight left in me to get us out of this. I'm sorry."

"I think we should go with them," Cap said. "So long as I'm here, nothing bad will happen to any of you, I promise."

"I'm holding you to that," Stella said.

As the soldiers took them all into custody and packed them into a truck for transport, they confiscated Atria's sword. She was too exhausted and sore to even think of resisting.

Chapter XI – Conference

"How many unidentified cosplayers have died of
dehydration or exposure in the last ten years?"

Stella sat at a one of the tables in the Japanese Self-
Defence Force base conference room. At the door stood
two guards with rifles. To her right sat Adam, and to her
left were Atria and Captain Infinite. She looked at her
fiancé. He was fidgeting as he always did when he was
nervous. She took his hand and squeezed it.

"It will be okay," Stella said.

"We're foreigners," Adam said. "We have no legal
standing here. What's stopping them from just throwing us
in jail and tossing away the key?"

"That wouldn't happen," Cap said. "Under Japanese
law, if a foreigner is arrested the police have to inform
them of the suspected crime within 48 hours or let them
go. The longest they can keep you without charging you is
28 days, and to do that they have to get an extension from

a court of law. And these aren't the police anyway, so this isn't a criminal justice matter – at least not yet."

Everybody stared at Cap for a moment.

"What I do is adjacent to law enforcement," Cap explained. "You have to know what the laws are before you can even think of helping to enforce them. Besides, in a worst-case scenario I can just fly you back to Canada myself."

"I wish we had been allowed to go back to the hotel room first," Atria said. "I really want to get out of this uniform."

"I wish they hadn't taken our cell phones," Stella added. "Kaguyama and Mitsubi must be worried sick about us by now."

Footfalls sounded outside and the door opened. Stella looked up to see Kaguyama and Mitsubi ushered in and directed to sit at their table. Kaguyama glanced at the bloodstain on Atria's uniform as he sat down and went pale.

"What happened to you?" he asked.

"Fight didn't go well," Atria replied in Japanese. "Don't worry about it."

"You're my creation," Kaguyama said. "I'm allowed to worry." He looked at Cap. "Are you Captain Infinite?"

Cap nodded and smiled. "I guess I'm famous," he said in Japanese. "It is an honour to meet you."

"I'm Junichi Kaguyama," Kaguyama said. "I wrote Atria's light novel series. This is Aiko Mitsubi, my illustrator."

"It is an honour to meet you, Captain Infinite," Mitsubi said.

"Please, call me 'Cap'. All my friends do."

The guards snapped to attention as a party of officers entered the room, along with a man in a dark suit. The party took its seat at a facing table, a couple of the officers opening up laptops while one pulled out a paper file.

"Oh good, we can get started at last," Atria whispered.

One of the officers stood. "My name is Colonel Hajime Sato," he said in Japanese. "Commanding officer of the 47th Infantry Regiment of the Eastern Army. According to our files, you are Adam Jacobs and Anne Marie Sorenson of Kingston, Ontario, here on a tourist visa, and Junichi Kaguyama and Aiko Mitsubi, author and illustrator of *Eternal Chronicle of Hyperborea*. Mr. Jacobs and Ms. Sorenson have a moderate observed fluency in Japanese." He cocked his head as he read something in Kaguyama's file, and closed it. "The other two of you we have no file on, as you appear to be fictional characters, Captain Infinite from Superhero Comics and Atria Silversword from *Eternal Chronicle of Hyperborea*."

"That's 'Major'," Atria interjected. "I am Major Atria Silversword, commander of the 18th Mechanized Company in the 2nd Hyperborean Army. My world may be a fiction created by yours, but I am still a duly commissioned officer, and I have a rank that should be respected."

Colonel Sato looked at her for a moment and then bowed. "Apologies, Major. You are correct. Normally, we would find the idea of fictional characters coming to life unbelievable, but the implications from the CCTV footage from the altercation late this afternoon cannot be ignored."

Stella raised her hand. "She and Cap are not the only ones from a story. I'm Princess Stellaria from *Chronicles of Arcaniana*. I got to this world about five years ago."

The colonel glanced at the man in the suit and then back at her. "So you are in this country on falsified documents."

Stella opened her mouth to speak, but then looked down at the table. "I guess so," she muttered.

"You understand that we now have an obligation to contact your embassy and bring this to their attention,"

Sato said.

Stella stared at the table and didn't reply. She felt Adam take her hand and give it a squeeze. It wasn't comforting.

"Anyway, let us get everybody on the same page, as you foreigners like to say," Sato said. "On or about 16:00 hours local time this afternoon, Major Silversword, Mr. Jacobs, Princess Stellaria also known as Ms. Sorenson, and Captain Infinite were involved in an altercation with two unidentified individuals in the New Keihin Industrial Park, located in the Keihin Industrial Zone. This altercation quickly escalated to include large amounts of property damage across three city blocks."

"If I may," Captain Infinite interjected. "I may have been a latecomer to this incident, but I did hear it start. My friends here attempted to negotiate, but these negotiations failed. I do not believe they can be blamed for starting this fight."

Sato looked up from his notes. "Did you see this?"

Cap paused. "No sir, I only heard it. But my friends had a good reason for what they did."

"We'll get to that," Sato said. "Right now, we are just establishing the timeline of events. This altercation lasted approximately 35 minutes, during which time alarmed civilians in the area contacted the authorities. At 16:21 hours my unit was deployed to secure the area under the authority of the internal security and public order provisions of the 1954 Self-Defense Forces Act. The area was reported secured at 16:49. Major Silversword, Captain Infinite, Mr. Jacobs, and Princess Stellaria AKA Ms. Sorenson were apprehended at 16:54 without incident. The two unidentified participants in this altercation were not located or apprehended. Based on information from initial debriefings with Major Silversword and Princess Stellaria AKA Ms. Sorenson, men were sent to apprehend Mr.

Kaguyama and Ms. Mitsubi, which also occurred without incident. Are there any disagreements as to these facts?"

"I want to know why we were apprehended," Kaguyama said.

"It's okay," Atria said. "They were just trying to minimize the variables in this situation. Now everybody is in the same location. I would have done the same."

"As I said, my friends here had good reason for what they did," Captain Infinite began. Colonel Sato raised his hand.

"Let's move on to preliminary estimates of property damage," Sato said. "In the affected area, two buildings have either partially or fully collapsed. Five buildings suffered sufficient structural damage to be declared unfit for human occupation, and have been deemed unrepairable. Three buildings have suffered sufficient structural damage to be declared unfit for human occupation, but are considered to be repairable. Four more buildings suffered minor structural damage, but have been deemed fit for continued occupation so long as repairs are completed within 14 days."

Captain Infinite stared at the table. "We may have gotten a bit carried away."

"It is a miracle that nobody was killed," Sato declared. "I trust I do not need to review the casualty figures to impress further upon you the seriousness of this situation. People were hurt. Now, my colleagues and I would like to know why fictional characters have appeared in the real world and fought a battle in the middle of Tokyo on a Saturday afternoon."

"I think that's you, my love," Adam whispered in Stella's ear.

Stella stood. "Sir, I am a graduate student of quantum physics at Queen's University, and my research area is directly connected to my appearance in this world five years ago. I think I can answer at least some of your questions, but I do have to caution you that this material is very complicated, and may not be understandable to lay persons."

"Please, indulge us," Sato said.

Stella took a deep breath. "Very well. Every single sub-atomic particle has what we call 'information'. A good way of thinking of this is that each particle is stamped with documentation of every quantum state it has ever existed in. The ability to interact with this information is the basis of quantum computing theory.

"My research suggests that information can contain much more than just the present and past states of the particle in question. If this particle comes from the neurons of the human brain, it can also encode the ideas and concepts the person was thinking about when that neuron fired. When enough people think about the same ideas, such as the setting of a popular story, this information reaches a critical mass, turning it into a physical place – effectively creating an alternate reality based on the encoded information."

Stella looked around the room. Nobody looked lost yet. Good. "These realities are not independent. They are linked back to the world that created them – this world – by what I call an 'information stream'. As new additions are made by the creators of this world and people read or see them, they travel down the information stream and are manifested in the created world as a physical reality.

"Up until the last hundred years or so, this transit was only one-way. What was possible in the created world and the information stream itself was governed by what was thought to be possible by those consuming the stories in question. So, information could move down the information stream to the created world, but not back."

"What changed?" Sato asked.

"In 1912, an American author named Edgar Rice Burroughs published a novel titled *A Princess of Mars*," Stella replied. "This story involved a character travelling from one world to another. As Burroughs' *Mars* stories became more and more successful, the idea of being able to travel between worlds entered the information streams generated by anybody who had read it, regardless of what story they were reading at any given time. With travelling between worlds as a possibility now encoded into the information streams, they became two-way – under very rare circumstances, a person from one of these created worlds could accidentally fall into the information stream and arrive here, in the world that created them."

"Wait," the man in the suit said, speaking for the first time. In her peripheral vision, she saw Captain Infinite blink in surprise. "So you are saying that characters have been coming out of stories into the real world for the last *hundred* years?"

Stella nodded. "It is almost a certainty. Once the path was opened, people started falling through it."

"Why haven't we known about this?" Sato asked. "Why is an altercation like this just happening now?"

"For one thing, there is a disconnect between the laws of physics here and those of the created worlds," Stella replied. "When one of us transits the information stream, we carry with us a bubble of the physics of our world. This allows us to use abilities that would otherwise break this world's laws of physics, at least for a short while. But, the longer we are here, the more that bubble fades. Within a year, there is no functional difference between a person from a created world and somebody who was born in this one.

"For another, most of us who fall into this world probably don't survive long enough for anybody to notice us. When we arrive in this world, we are shocked and alone and confused. We don't know anything works, who might be friend or foe, or sometimes even what we can eat or burn for warmth. Those who come from created worlds similar enough to this one to avoid the confusion probably survive long enough to integrate, but they just blend in."

"You're saying that characters from fiction have just been coming into our world for decades and dying without anybody noticing them?" the man in the suit asked, disbelief in his eyes.

Stella nodded. "How many unidentified cosplayers have died of dehydration or exposure in the last ten years?"

"Back to the main subject of concern," Colonel Sato interrupted, "why is an altercation like this happening here and now?"

"If I had to guess, it's because of the *isekai* genre," Stella replied. "People travelling between worlds has become a stable of Japanese pop culture and literature. This, in turn, finds its way into the information stream, making it easier for somebody to either fall into it by accident or travel along it deliberately, which is what our opponent has been doing. If you want to look at it another way, the gate that used to be open just a crack is now wide open."

Sato nodded. "Thank you. We would appreciate you putting this in writing for us. English is fine – we have our own translators."

Stella sat back on her chair, hoping that nobody had noticed her legs shaking. She closed her eyes and took a deep breath to calm herself.

"Now, what was this fight about?" Sato asked.

Atria stood up. "My turn. Approximately three days ago, an unidentified thief arrived in my world and stole a power source from one of our power generation facilities. We were attempting to recover this power source and return it to our world before the containment system on it fails. According to Captain Infinite, this failure has already begun."

"And if containment fails?"

"The blast would be approximately thirty to forty kilotons."

For a moment, Stella thought she saw Colonel Sato become stony-faced, but then it passed.

"I see," he said. "Do you know how long it will be before containment reaches critical failure?"

Atria shook her head. "Not at this time, sir."

"And should you acquire this power source, do you have a means for returning it to your world?"

"Not at this time, sir," Atria replied. "We had hoped to convince the thief to take it back himself, but our attempt to persuade him failed."

"And are you able at this time to identify this thief or his accomplice?" Sato said.

Beside Stella, Adam raised his hand. Sato saw him and nodded as Atria sat back in her chair. "We can identify the teenager," Adam stated. "Her name is Jenny Calhoun. She's from a series called *Jenny Calhoun, Monster Slayer* – at least that's what it is called in my country. I think her creator is appearing at the convention we came here to see. As far as I know, one of Captain Infinite's writers is there too."

"What about the thief?" Sato asked.

"None of us know who he is or where he's from. I'm sorry."

Sato took a deep breath. "I see." He turned to Cap. "Captain Infinite, your quality is well known in this country. You are the only Western comic book superhero to my knowledge who has retained all of their moral integrity. So, I ask you this: do you vouch for these people?"

"I do," Cap replied.

"Colonel Sato," Atria said, standing again. "As a duly commissioned officer and representative of the Hyperborean Army, I officially request the assistance of your government and military in the recovery of my nation's property."

"I am not authorized to grant such a request at this time," Sato said. "But I will take it up with my commanding officer and the Ministry. In the meantime, you will all be confined to barracks here on the base while we sort out this rather impressive mess."

"We were supposed to be attending a convention this weekend," Adam said. "There's still tomorrow–"

"You'll be missing that," Sato stated. "Captain Infinite, we are all aware that we can do nothing to prevent you from leaving this place if you so choose. We are, however, going respectfully request that you stay in confinement of your own free will while we resolve this matter."

"I will stay with my friends," Cap said.

"Very well," Sato said, standing. His party followed him. "This meeting is adjourned. The Sergeant first class will make arrangements for any belongings you require to be transported from your places of residence to the barracks. Otherwise, you will be informed of any decisions regarding this matter once they have been made."

As the officers left the room, Stella gripped her fiancé's hand and wondered what would happen next.

Chapter XII – Confinement

"They arrested us and told us this unbelievable story
about fictional characters coming to life."

By the time they made it to their assigned barracks, it was
already past 11:00 at night. Over two dozen bunk beds
lined the walls, but they seemed to have the place to
themselves. Atria took the opportunity of a free water
closet and a borrowed set of fatigues to change out of her
blood-crusted uniform. When she came out, she found Cap
approaching Stella and Adam.

"Stella," Cap said. "I've got a question about what you
said in the meeting."

"What is it?" Stella asked.

"So, I get that if I stay here, my powers are going to
fade," Cap started. "So, I'll lose my ability to fly and shoot
lasers from my eyes. But what about things like strength
and longevity? I mean, I'm not human to begin with – I fell

through a dimensional portal into my world."

"I'm sorry," Stella said. "I just don't know. You'll lose any ability that breaks the laws of physics, but I don't think anything else would be affected."

Cap looked slightly unhappy about the answer. "Well, thanks anyway. I'm going to go see if they brought me the street clothes I requested after the meeting."

After Cap wandered off, she saw Adam give Stella a hug and kiss and make his way to the water closet. Stella sat down on the lower bed and buried her head in her hands.

"Are you okay?" Atria asked, stepping over. Stella looked up, her eyes red.

"I'll be fine," Stella said.

"I'm sure the thing with your documents will get sorted out," Atria said.

Stella smiled, her eyes sad. "It's not that. Well, it's not just that. When the battle started, I was completely useless."

"From what you said in the debriefing, your bluff distracted the thief long enough for Cap to show up. I would have died if that hadn't happened."

"Five years ago, I would have rained destruction on his head," Stella said. "I would have been able to paralyze him in place, or put a magical barrier between you and one of those spikes of his. That's all gone now."

Atria took a deep breath. "Stella, I don't want to ever hear you say that you're useless again. Not ever."

"But it's true."

"Why?" Atria demanded. "Because you can't fight on the front lines anymore? Because you can't do what you used to be able to do? Everybody goes through that. I'm going to go through that. There's already things I used to be able to do as a teenager that I can't do now. You're not the same person you were five years ago. In five years you're not going to be the same person you are right now. That's just life.

"You may not have noticed this, but there was a grand total of *one* person in that conference room who had any understanding of why any of this is happening, and that's *you*. There's only one person who has any chance of unravelling all this and getting us home, and that's *you*. There's only one person who those officers are going to turn to for answers, and that's *you*. And there's only one person with enough experience to be a good candidate for first contact with others like us who fall into this world, and that's *you*. If a battle starts, you are the only person in this barracks who isn't expendable. There is nothing Cap and I can do that can't be replicated with enough firepower. You are irreplaceable."

Stella gave her a fragile smile. "Thank you for saying that."

"It's all true," Atria said. "Leave the fighting to Cap and me – you worry about doing the things that only you can do." She saw Adam returning from the water closet. "I'll leave you in the hands of your fiancé."

Atria grabbed the lower bunk beside Stella's and fluffed her pillow. On the other side, Kaguyama and Mitsubi were discussing who would take the top bunk bed. Kaguyama glanced at Atria, and just as quickly glanced away.

Atria sighed. "It's okay," she told him in Japanese. "I don't hate you for what you said."

Kaguyama looked at her. "You have every right to."

"I imagine I do," she stated. "But I don't. I'm an officer in a combat unit – I've sent men to their deaths in diversionary attacks. I imagine what you do is the same. I'm not happy about it, and I don't know if I ever will be. But, I know there isn't any malice in it. You do what you need to in order to tell a good story, and I'm just one of the pieces you use to do it."

"That's not true," Kaguyama said. "You're not just a game piece to me, and you never have been. None of my characters are. You're all like the children I never had. I know everything about you – every triumph, every setback, everything. The same goes for Abel, and everybody else in your story. I know how much it hurt you when Abel died, but I cried when I wrote it too. You lost your best friend, and I lost a surrogate son. But that was where the story went, and that was what it required."

Atria nodded and settled back in her bunk. "We should all get some sleep. Tomorrow could be a busy day."

The next morning they found their luggage waiting just inside the door to the barracks. Included were some street clothes for Captain Infinite – a button down shirt, sports jacket, and slacks. Cap held up the clothes and grinned. "Just what I asked for," he said.

Once everybody had finished using the water closet and getting changed, Atria sat on her bed and took stock. Regardless of what happened today, she needed to check her antigrav unit. Her pistol was almost certainly a lost cause – even if it could be located among the rubble from the battle, it wasn't designed to withstand a building falling on it. She'd also need a new uniform jacket, at the very least – her street clothes were good for now, but if she was going to represent her nation to the Japanese Army, she needed to be properly attired.

The door opened, and a couple of orderlies walked in with a large folding table and a meal cart. Quiet and polite, they set up the table and laid out breakfast, then saluted and left. Atria and the others sat down.

"I've been wondering," Atria said to Adam in English, "how did you two meet? I've heard Stella's side, but I would love to know yours."

"I found her mostly starved in an alleyway on my way home from school," Adam said. "She claimed to be a character from a video game I had been playing. So, I asked her for proof."

"And she showed you a spell, right?"

Adam shook his head. "She tried, but she was too weak. Nothing happened."

Beside Adam, Stella startled.

"But she seemed so convinced of it," Adam continued, "and so desperate, that I made a leap of faith and took her home with me. I got my proof a couple of days later when Stella tried to fetch something from a tall shelf with magic, and accidentally brought down everything on it."

Atria nodded. They sat and ate in silence for a couple of minutes.

"Not bad for army food," Kaguyama said in Japanese after swallowing. "They've gotten better since I my time."

"You were in the army?" Mitsubi asked.

Kaguyama nodded. "Just for three years after school."

"That explains all those military terms we had trouble understanding in the anime," Adam said.

"You write what you know," Kaguyama stated. "And I wanted to write a military science fiction story that got things right."

They ate in silence for another minute.

"Well, this brings back memories," Atria said in Japanese, smiling.

"What, being in barracks?" Stella asked.

Atria shook her head. "Being *confined* to barracks."

Stella perked up. "What happened?"

"So, for any unit in training, the final exercise before graduation is to take on another training unit in live-fire field manoeuvres, using training rounds," Atria explained. "At least, that's what everybody in the unit is told. In reality, you're put up against one of the elite combat units. The army wants to give you a bloody nose and knock some of the arrogance out of you, you see. So, the fact that you are up against an elite unit is a closely guarded secret that the trainees should never, ever discover."

"And you did," Stella said.

Atria grinned. "Somebody told us about it, yes. So, the night before the exercise, someone – and I'm not saying it was me – snuck into the depot and someone – and I'm not saying it was me – replaced all of the opposing force's training rounds with weighted foam. So when the exercise started, our unit was the only one firing any live rounds. The CO was *pissed*. Our entire unit was confined to barracks for one week. They were so annoyed at us that they forgot to swear us to secrecy right after the exercise was done, so we tipped off the next class. Worth it, though, especially since it took us three hours to finish spray painting all that foam. That was the first time I was confined."

Stella and the others laughed. "What was the second?" Stella said.

"Well, two years later it was our combat unit's turn to go up against the graduating class. And, just in case the word was still spreading about what the exercise really was and somebody decided to do something about it, I went into the depot and checked our training rounds. All spray-painted foam."

"But you didn't report it," Stella guessed.

"Absolutely not! Our unit got together, and replaced all of *their* training rounds with foam too. It needs to be a fair fight after all." Atria laughed. "Both units were confined to barracks for two weeks. That was the last year they used those training rounds. I think they shifted to a laser targeting system after that."

Kaguyama chuckled. "I remember writing that. It was

fun. One of the best parts of volume three."

"It was volume two," Mitsubi said. "Remember?"

Kaguyama closed his eyes. "Ah yes, you're right. Sorry. I mis-remembered."

"Was it based on real life?" Atria asked. "Did you do something like that?"

Kaguyama shook his head. "The army didn't do that sort of thing when I went through training. I just thought it would be a good idea if they did, so I put it into your story and let you react to it. It was the first time your character surprised me, and the moment I knew you had truly come to life."

"I actually drew you painting the rounds," Mitsubi said. "I could show you that when this is over, if you want."

Atria nodded. "I think I'd like that very much. It's one of my fondest memories."

The door opened and a pair of orderlies entered the room holding luggage. Behind them were two newcomers, carrying duffle bags and looking annoyed. One was an African American woman of medium height and stature with curly hair, and the other was a slightly overweight grey-haired caucasian man.

Cap waved at them. "Welcome to our little hotel," he said in English, shifting over to make room at the table. "Plenty of food left, if you want some."

The orderlies put down the luggage, bowed and left, closing the door behind them.

"They arrested us and told us this unbelievable story about fictional characters coming to life," the man said. "Do any of you know about this?"

Cap grinned. "Well, I'm Captain Infinite, but all my friends call me 'Cap', and I hope you will too. That there is Princess Stella, and there is Major Atria Silversword. The others are Atria's author Junichi Kaguyama, and her illustrator Aiko Mitsubi. They don't speak English, but both Atria and I are fluent in Japanese, so we can translate if needed."

The two newcomers looked at each other for a moment in disbelief. "Shouldn't you be in costumes or something?" the woman asked.

Atria swallowed what she had been chewing. "My uniform got wrecked in battle the other day. I'm waiting to arrange a new one."

"I stopped fitting in my outfit three years and fifteen pounds ago," Stella said. She looked at Adam. "Maybe I should try to trim down a bit before the wedding."

"I only wear the tights when I'm working," Cap added. "They're in a duffel bag by the bunk, if you want to see them. I don't mind. Just don't lose them."

"Seriously," the man said. "Can you prove *any* of this?"

Cap stood up. "Yeah, sure. Just give me a bit of space – this is the sort of thing I usually do outside, with lots of clearance." Slowly and gingerly, he rose to hover a foot off the ground. Then he glided down the line of beds. At the end of the row, he landed and walked back to the newcomers and held out his hand. "As I said, I'm Captain Infinite. It's a pleasure to meet you."

Both of the newcomer's eyes turned cold. Neither took his hand. "Good for you," the man said. "I'm Mark Gable. I write comic books."

"I'm Alice Matson," the woman said. "I'm the showrunner and creator of *Jenny Calhoun, Monster Slayer*." The both moved past Cap and sat at the table away from his plate.

Beside Atria, Stella blinked in surprise. "What's that all about?" she whispered in Atria's ear.

"I don't know," Atria whispered back. She turned to Alice Matson and Mark Gable. "Look, we know this is hard to take in, but we can all vouch for Cap. He personally saved the life of Stella, Adam, and me, and he doesn't have a malicious bone in his body."

Cap sat back at his plate. "It's okay, Atria," he said, his voice subdued. "They don't have any obligation to like me, or anybody else they don't want to. You can't force people to be your friend."

"No, it's not okay," Atria retorted, staring at Mark and Alice. "You just snubbed a worthy comrade in battle and one of the best men I have ever met. Which is far more than I can say for your Jenny Calhoun, who is quite the vicious little psychopath."

Alice blinked and shook her head. "Wait, Jenny Calhoun is here, just like you are?"

"Out there somewhere," Atria declared. "She nearly killed me, and if she had succeeded she was going to kill my friend Stella next because I had 'annoyed her'. And she really likes the word 'stabby' for some reason. So considering what your creation is up to, I don't think you have any justification for snubbing Cap. He's right that I can't force you to like him, but while I am around you *will* respect him!"

Alice looked down at the table and swallowed. "I never wrote her to be that way. Angsty, yes, but not vicious."

"Well, she's that way now," Atria said, turning and lifting her shirt to display the scar on her side. "She's the one who did this to me." She lowered the shirt and returned to her food.

Alice closed her eyes for a moment. "For whatever Jenny has done, I am so very sorry."

"Just treat Cap with respect, okay?"

"Okay," Alice muttered.

Breakfast finished in an awkward silence. Once it was done, Atria went to her bunk, pulled the belt and antigrav out of her duffel bag, and brought it to the table. Out of a pouch on the belt she pulled out a small screwdriver set and started opening up the back of the antigrav.

Kaguyama and Mitsubi sat down on each side of her. "I've never seen the inside of one of these before," Mitsubi said in Japanese. "May we?"

"Sure," Atria replied. "Just don't touch anything." She opened up the back. Everything looked like it was where it should be.

"So what happened?" Kaguyama asked.

"These aren't built to handle being slammed into the sides of buildings," Atria said. "So when that happened, it stopped working. Everything looks right...hopefully the shock just jostled the battery for a moment, and it will be fine."

"And if it doesn't work anyway?" Mitsubi said.

Atria closed the unit up. "Then it's broken. I'm a combat officer, not an engineer." She grabbed the pillow from her bed and wrapped the belt and antigrav around it. "Stella, could I get your help for a moment?"

Stella looked up from where she had been sitting with Adam and Cap. "Sure. What do you need?"

Atria held up the pillow. "Just stop this, very carefully. If it's travelling upwards, just let it go to the ceiling. The antigrav is rated to lift up to 350 pounds." She turned on the antigrav, held the pillow in front of her, and then let it go. The pillow floated in the air.

"So far, so good," Atria muttered, tapping the pillow in Stella's direction. It glided towards Stella. Stella caught it with a delighted grin.

"You could make a really fun game out of this," Stella said.

"Stella, I'm shocked," Atria declared. "This is an expensive piece of military hardware. I would never use it for such a frivolous purpose." Her face broke into a grin.

"At least, not during on-duty hours. Unfortunately, we just have the one, and it's already taken at least one shock. So, we'll have to use it sparingly. Send it back, please."

After Atria recovered the pillow, she turned the antigrav off and recovered her belt. All that was left to do was wait.

She spent a while just sitting by the window and watching. Mitsubi was examining Cap's tights and peppering him with questions about it. Kaguyama had sat down at the table, opened his laptop, and started writing. Alice and Mark sat uncomfortably on their beds, no doubt trying to make sense of it all. Stella and Adam sat nearby, chatting, with Stella occasionally offering to let Atria join them. She waved her off. Sometimes it was good to enjoy the quiet moments.

It was a couple of hours after lunch that the door opened and Colonel Sato entered with one of his officers, making his way over to her. Atria stood and greeted him.

"Your request for assistance has been considered by my superiors and the Ministry," Sato said in Japanese.

"And?"

"It is granted. We will help you."

Atria nodded and thanked him. The waiting was over. It was time to get to work.

Chapter XIII – Unexpected Meetings

"I want to meet my creator and hold him to account for
the world he created."

The bank guards Jenny had killed now appeared in her
nightmares. At least, they did in the handful of hours that
Jenny was able to sleep.

The guards screamed and begged for mercy. Behind
them, the shadowy figures of their wives and children
pleaded with her. She wanted to turn and reply, but her
knives were already moving and killing. She tried to stop,
but her arms moved of their own accord. As each guard
fell to her knives, their loved ones fell to their knees and
sobbed. She opened her mouth to apologize, to explain, to
say something, *anything*, but nothing came out.

She startled awake in The Destroyer's arms, breathing
heavily. Tears ran down her cheeks. The abandoned
warehouse they had turned into their new base was silent.

"You were having a nightmare," The Destroyer said.
"You wanted me to hold you when that happened."

Jenny nodded and buried her face in his robes. "I killed those people," she muttered.

"You said that they didn't matter because they weren't real," The Destroyer said. "Why does it cause you such distress if they're fictional like us?"

"They aren't real," Jenny sobbed. "And it doesn't matter. It *shouldn't* matter. But I can't stop seeing their faces! Why can't I stop seeing their faces?"

Jenny wiped the tears away. She couldn't afford them. Their enemies had shown themselves, and one was not only a superhero, but *the* superhero, Captain Infinite himself. She had watched him throw The Destroyer around like a rag doll. And then there was that anime girl, who had proven to be at least as strong as she was. And when Jenny had her knife to the anime girl's throat...she had hesitated.

Jenny shook her head. Why had she hesitated? She hadn't hesitated with the bank guards. She hadn't hesitated with all the monsters she had fought back in her own world. But she had hesitated here, against an enemy who would never have done so had their positions been reversed. If anime girl had her dead to rights, Jenny would be dead.

Jenny sighed. "I was made broken, Roy."

"Feeling things doesn't mean you're broken," The Destroyer said. "I think you're human. I'm the one with all of the gaps in my mind – *that's* being made broken."

"I want to know why I'm this way," Jenny said. "I want to find the one who created me and ask her why she made me and everybody I care about suffer. I want to know why she hated me."

"I will help you do that if you want," The Destroyer said.

Jenny looked up into his eyes. "And what about you? Don't you want to meet your creator and find out why he made you the way he did? Don't you want him to give you a name?"

The Destroyer stared at her for a moment. "I think I want to know why I don't have a name. I think I want to find my creator."

"Let's do that, then," Jenny declared. "Let's find our creators, and find out why they made us what we are."

"That's an admirable goal," a midwestern American voice said from the shadows. "But a bit harder to make a reality, I think."

Jenny was crouched in a combat stance with her knives drawn before she was even aware she had moved. "Who are you?"

A tall man with short dark hair, wearing a black three-piece suit, stepped into the open. "My name is Jack Death. You visited my world. I was quite impressed with what you left behind."

"What do you want?" Jenny demanded.

"To discuss joining you," Jack said. "I saw your fight with Captain Infinite and the woman in the green uniform. A girl and a wizard against a living god seemed to be an unfair contest. I don't like those."

"Why do you want to join us?" The Destroyer asked. "What do you gain?"

"I want to meet my creator and hold him to account for the world he created."

"So you know we're all fictional characters," Jenny said, sheathing her knives and rising from her combat stance, "that our lives were created to amuse the people of this world."

"It didn't take long to figure out," Jack stated. "My world is empty and simplistic compared to this one. All I had to do was sit in a park and watch people to see the difference. There's so many different kinds of people here, leading so many different lives. They do things I don't

105

understand, but I want to. They live in such unfathomable peace. All my world has ever had is violence, and I am never going back there."

Jenny watched Jack pause for a moment. Then he added, "And, I think, if I kill my creator, I'll kill the way back as well."

"Your world does not make you happy?" The Destroyer asked.

Jack shrugged. "I don't know what 'happy' even means. When I remove an obstacle, I feel satisfaction. When somebody makes a demand, I feel trepidation. When I fight and kill, I feel nothing. I thought that was normal, until I got here. When people smile in this world, there isn't any malice in their eyes. That's not normal, at least where I'm from."

"Your world sounds worse than mine," Jenny said, "which is quite impressive. My story turned my world into a hellscape in which I lost everybody I ever cared about or loved. But at least I had those people in the first place."

"I will champion your cause," The Destroyer declared. "You may join us. I would see you learn what it is to be happy."

Jenny held out her hand. "Welcome to the gang. I'm Jenny, and this is Roy."

Jack paused for a moment, and then took her hand and shook it.

"I am known as The Destroyer," The Destroyer added. "'Roy' is what Jenny has decided to call me."

"His creator was so half-assed that he didn't even bother giving Roy an actual name," Jenny explained. "But as I keep telling him, Roy is not a villain and doesn't deserve the title he has."

"From what I saw in the bank," Jack said, "the title isn't completely wrong."

"Maybe," Jenny said. "But I spent my life hunting and

fighting monsters. I know the real monsters when I see them. Roy isn't one. He's just a good man with horns on his head and magic powers."

"You've still got a problem, though," Jack said. "Captain Infinite. He and his friends want that orb of yours, whatever it is, and they'll kill you to get it. I know killers when I see them. It's why you're hiding here and not just staying in a hotel. What is that orb thing, anyway?"

"It's a power source," The Destroyer replied. "It maintains my powers in this world, and allows me to travel to other worlds at will."

"So why not hide in one of those?"

The Destroyer smiled, his eyes beaming with enthusiasm. "I like this one the best. All the others are empty in comparison. And this is the world where our creators are, so it is where we need to be. It is the place that makes me happy." He looked at Jenny for a moment. "It is the place I hope my friend can be happy and at peace."

"Makes sense," Jack said. "I can probably hold the woman in the military uniform at bay with my guns, but they won't do anything against Captain Infinite. The man's bulletproof. And knife-proof. And, although you haven't seen it yet, he can shoot lasers out of his eyes. I'm amazed you managed to get a hit in on him at all, and he recovered very quickly. We're going to need more help."

Jenny nodded. "I know. We know of him in my world too. How overpowered do you have to be that you're famous in worlds that aren't even related to your story?"

"So, we need to know what our enemies are doing, what they're planning, and where we can recruit allies."

"I can help with that," The Destroyer said. "I am not without the powers of a god myself. I will scrye for the answers."

The Destroyer waved his hand in a flourish. Four images appeared in the air before him. Jenny's eyes widened. In the first, the people who had fought them languished in what appeared to be a barracks. In the second, a black woman was being escorted by Japanese soldiers alongside a slightly overweight grey-haired white guy to the door of a long building. In the third, a short Japanese man in a bathrobe tapped away at a keyboard in a small apartment. And in the fourth, a tall Japanese man with a scar on his face in a blue cloak and leather armour leaned against a wall, shaking his head.

"Our enemies are in confinement," The Destroyer reported. "They have requested the aid of the government of this nation, but that request has not yet been approved. Jenny's creator has been taken into custody and is being confined with them. Her name is Alice Matson. My creator lives at the other end of this city. His name is Habiki Matoyami. And a new character has fallen into this world, and is in a city called Osaka. His name is Daiki Yamato, and he seeks his family."

"Then we need to take advantage of our enemies being sidelined and get to Daiki Yamato before they do," Jack stated. "We recruit him, and then find and meet our creators."

"That works for me," Jenny said. "Once we've got this new guy in our camp, we'll meet Roy's creator first. We know he's unprotected."

The Destroyer waved his hand again. The images dissolved into the air. "Then we have an agreement." He paused. "Does anybody know where Osaka is?"

Chapter XIV – Daiki Yamato

"My family and I have lived here for the last twenty-five years."

Daiki Yamato leaned against an alley wall and tried to process what had happened. A couple of people passed by, pointing at his clothes in appreciation and saying something about admiring his cosplay. Daiki waved them off.

He had started that morning in the village that he called home with Athena, the half-wolf demi-human he loved and who had guarded him as his shield ever since he had saved her from slavers, shortly after arriving in her world. The Devil King's forces had paused for the moment, regrouping, and allowing his party a short period of peace. The other two Legendary Weapon Heroes and their parties were somewhere far across the countryside looking for mystical artifacts or the like to make themselves stronger, which suited Daiki just fine – he couldn't stand being around the idiots. After all, they were the ones who had supported the false theft allegation that psychopath Saline had used to destroy his life for the better part of a year.

He and Athena had been enjoying a romantic walk, talking about their upcoming wedding, when the ground had given way underneath him. That wasn't right – it hadn't so much given way as just stopped existing. The last thing he heard was Athena's anguished scream of his name and then he was here, in this alley.

But...

Across the street from the mouth of the alley, a vendor was selling udon noodles and pressed sushi, and he could smell the batter of an *okonomikyaki* cake frying down the street. The passers-by spoke in a distinct Kansai dialect. Every now and then the sound of a busy sea port rose above the din of the street.

There was no mistaking it. This was Japan. Not only was it Japan, it was Osaka.

He was home.

Daiki leaned against the wall and took a deep breath, cursing whatever gods had brought him here. For the second time, he had been torn away from people he loved and dropped into another world. Once again, he had no way back. He might have been transported home, but without Athena what did it matter? And this cursed Black Sword was still stuck to him, always on his person.

But, even if Athena wasn't here with him, he was still home. He could see his parents again for the first time in a year and a half. Perhaps they'd be able to say something that could comfort him, or at least put him up until he could figure out what to do.

Daiki stepped out of the alley and checked the street signs. He nodded to himself – it would be a long walk to get back to the house he grew up in, but after a year and a half in Athena's world, he had grown used to those. Besides, without any Japanese money, he didn't have any other options. He'd just have to put up with the people wanting to snap pictures of him with their phones.

As he walked through the streets towards his home, he tried to remember his mother's laugh and his father's smile, but it was Athena's face that he kept coming back to instead. Athena, who he would never see again. He tightened his fist, ignoring a couple of schoolgirls who pointed and talked at him. His parents. He'd get to see his parents. That was what was important now. He could feel sad about losing Athena later.

He turned a corner into the residential area. The house he grew up in was only a couple of blocks away. A memory of walking down some of these streets to school flickered in his mind. He was almost home.

And then he came to the house he grew up in.

The colour was just as he remembered it. Pale brick on the first floor, with white walls framing the windows on the second. An unfamiliar car sat in the driveway, but his parents were probably overdue for a new one anyway. He took a deep breath and then paused. Should he knock? Open the front door and go right in? Just how do you approach your parents when you've been missing for a year and a half?

Daiki took another deep breath. He would knock. No assumptions. For all he knew, they wouldn't be home yet anyway. He stepped up to the front door and knocked. His breath caught as he heard footsteps approach. The door opened.

A complete stranger stood in the doorframe, looking at him.

He was in his mid-fifties, by the look of it, short and clean-shaven. His eyes looked up and down Daiki's leather armour and blue cloak, but his face betrayed no emotion.

"Can I help you?" he asked politely.

"Um, yes," Daiki said. "I'm looking for somebody who used to live here, I guess. The Yamato family. I grew up in this house. I was wondering if you know where they might have gone after you bought the place."

"I'm afraid you must be mistaken," the man said. "My family and I have lived here for the last twenty-five years."

Daiki swallowed. "I see. You must be correct – I've got the wrong house. Thank you for your time."

"Are you okay, young man?" the man said. "You look pale."

"It's nothing," Daiki said, turning and starting to walk away. "Thank you for your concern."

Daiki made it two blocks before his composure failed. He leaned against a lamppost, slid down it to the sidewalk, and wept. It was the wrong Japan. It had happened again. First he had been torn away from his family and thrust into a world where he was forced to fight a war for people who accused him of theft and hated him. Then, when he had finally found a reason to fight for that world and a woman he wanted to spend the rest of his life with, he had been torn away from her and dropped here.

Was there no end to the cruelty of the gods?

He was vaguely aware of people passing by. Some made a show of ignoring him. Others stopped and asked if he was alright, or offered to help. Those he waved off. Finally, he had no tears left to cry. He took a ragged breath and collected himself.

He was alone, but he was also alive, and that was something. And, it was possible that Athena had also fallen into this world behind him. If she had, he needed to find her. And if she was here, she would be looking for him too. It was a faint hope, but it could be enough, at least for the moment.

So, he needed to be able to look for her. And for that

he needed money and a place to stay. The coinage he carried was gold and silver – if he was lucky, it was still early enough for him to get to a place where he could sell it. And then he would need to find a hostel. He could worry about clothing and supplies tomorrow.

He got up and began walking. If Athena was here, he would find her. That was his mission. And if she wasn't...

He couldn't finish the thought.

Gritting his teeth, he continued on his way downtown.

Chapter XV – Revelations

"I can't give you your happy ending."

Captain Infinite and Adam sat on a couch in the barracks lounge, watching anime on television. As Adam tried to explain what was on the screen, Cap felt as though his brains were going to melt out of his ears.

"So, let me get this straight," Cap said, taking a sip from a glass of water and putting it down on the coffee table. "The magical knights flying around in the last show *aren't* superhoes."

"Correct."

"But the normal guys in costumes that give them super-strength and abilities *are*."

"That's right."

"But the magical people who can fly around and throw fire at one another *aren't* superheroes."

"That's correct."

"That makes no sense to me," Cap said.

"Different culture, different idea of superheroes," Adam said.

Cap shrugged. "I guess so. I think I like the magical knights more than the guys in costumes. Just one more question, though: the red-haired magical knight – why does she need a battle mech?"

Adam was about to answer when Cap saw Alice Matson walk into the lounge on the other side of the room. He stood up and called out, "Alice, can I ask you a question?"

Alice rolled her eyes. "Fine, just make it quick."

"Did I do something to offend you? If I did, could you tell me what it is so that I can make it right?"

"You really want to know?" Alice snapped.

Cap nodded. "Yes, I think I do."

Adam stood. "I'll leave you two alone," he said, leaving the room.

Cap watched Alice stare at him, and then take a deep breath. "It's because you are precisely the type of terrible character I detest!" she declared. "You're pure wish fulfilment! You have so many superpowers that it is a physical impossibility to challenge you without shoving some Ultratonium up your ass. Nobody can hurt you. Nobody can stop you. Good writing is all about narrative tension, and the moment you show up in a scene, that tension is gone. Nobody can even hide anything from you, because you've got a superpower that allows you to see through walls! Characters are compelling because of struggle and growth, but you're already a god among us, so you've got nowhere to go and no way to get there even if you did.

"*My* character, Jenny Calhoun, is out there right now and I wish to God I could find her. In the show I wrote for her, she had to struggle for every victory, and she had to suffer lots of loss and defeat to get there. That's what made her compelling, and made people keep watching every season. They wanted to see her beat the odds and win. God only knows what she thinks of me. But I don't get to spend time with her. Instead, I've got you. When was the last victory you had to earn?"

Cap sat down and sighed. "You're not wrong," he said quietly.

Alice cocked her head and stepped closer. "What did you just say?"

Cap stared up at her. "I said you're not wrong. You're right – I spend my days fighting people who never stand a chance against me, unless they somehow get their hands on Ultratonium, which they almost never do. Sometimes I even float there and lecture them after I've stopped them, which, when you think about it, is really easy to do when you're bulletproof and they're not. But what you're missing is that that's all I ever get to do."

Alice sat on an adjacent couch. "What do you mean?"

"Do you see this glass of water?" Cap asked, picking it up and holding it in front of her. Alice nodded. "In order to drink this glass of water, I have to concentrate very carefully. If I squeeze it just the slightest bit too hard, the glass will shatter with enough force to send shards through concrete walls. Everything is like this for me. If I'm not careful opening a door, I'll rip it off its hinges and send it flying down the hall. You're right – I'm a god among men. But that means that I don't get to be a man, or have what men have. Falling into this world was the first time in ages that I've had a proper challenge, it's true, but it's also the first time in decades I've had friends or people to spend time with who just treat me like one of them. All I get to do is fight supervillains."

"But what about Janey Jamison, the intrepid reporter, or Billy Wilson, the photographer? Surely they're in your life."

Cap put down the glass and shook his head. "They're long gone. They got old, and I didn't. I'm the only one of us left now. And you can't have a real life anywhere when you never age and everybody else does. I fight supervillains, and then I go to my cabin and watch television, and envy all the people on the screen for what they can have and I never could."

"But you have that secret identity to protect–"

Cap held up his hand. "I'm Captain Infinite, the Man of Titanium. Do I really seem like somebody who needs a secret identity to protect my friends? I put it on sometimes because when I do, if I'm very lucky, I might just be treated like one of you...for a short while, anyway." He sighed. "I would trade every single one of these powers you hate in a heartbeat just to be one of you for a day."

Alice looked down at her hands. "I'm sorry, I didn't realize."

Cap shrugged. "It's okay. When all anybody ever sees is the heroics, how can you know what's going on underneath them?"

They sat in silence for a moment.

"It wasn't always like this, you know," Cap said. "Back when I first fell into my world from my home dimension, I just had superior strength and speed. The rest of the powers grew over time, until, well, you know. But, in those early years, life was pretty good. And, I even got to punch Hitler."

Alice chuckled. "What was that like?"

Cap grinned. "Satisfying. Very satisfying."

Alice laughed.

Atria sat back in her new office and enjoyed the mid-afternoon sun shining through the window. The Japanese

Self-Defence Force had issued it to her shortly after telling her that they would help. Her first requirement was a replacement uniform, so that she could properly represent her nation. That, she was told, would take two or three days. Her second was that they sort out Stella's documentation. To her delight, on *that* requirement they were already ahead of her.

On the other side of her desk, Stella was holding and staring at her new birth certificate and Japanese passport. "They gave me my name back," she said softly. "I never thought I'd be able to use my name like this again."

"They tell me that they're still in talks with the Canadian embassy to sort out your citizenship and university enrollment," Atria said. "That could take a couple of weeks. It's an odd situation, or so they say."

Stella got up and gave her a hug. "Thank you so much. I was so worried I would never be allowed to go home with Adam at the end."

"Well, we have Cap in our corner," Atria stated. "In a worst-case scenario, he'd probably just fly you back to Canada himself. But, happily, that shouldn't be needed."

There was a knock at the door. Atria looked up to see Kaguyama and Mitsubi.

"Come in!" Atria called, switching to Japanese. "I have an office now! Mitsubi, while you're here, could I ask you for a favour?"

Mitsubi nodded. "Whatever you want."

"I've got no pictures to put on these walls. Could I get copies of some of the illustrations from the light novels? My friends, my mech, that sort of thing?"

Mitsubi grinned. "I think we can do that, yes."

Stella got up. "I'm going to go show this to Adam," she said, and left the room.

Atria glanced at Kaguyama. "So, are you finally going to sit down and tell me what has actually been bothering you this entire time?"

Kaguyama sat down. "You noticed."

"You wrote me to be an expert at reading people," Atria said. "And you're not that hard to read."

"Should I leave?" Mitsubi asked.

Kaguyama shook his head. "You have a right to know as well."

Atria sat back. "What is it?"

Kaguyama took a deep breath. "I can't give you your happy ending."

Atria blinked. "But I saw it in the outline. It was there."

"You don't understand," Kaguyama said. "I'm not going to be able to finish writing your story. I physically can't do it."

Atria leaned forward, reaching across the desk and taking Kaguyama's hand. "Please, tell me what is happening."

"I have early-onset Alzheimer's," Kaguyama said, hanging his head in shame. "It's why I missed all those deadlines."

Mitsubi gasped. "What?! When were you diagnosed with *that*?"

"About a year ago," Kaguyama replied. "I couldn't figure out how to tell anybody, and then Atria appeared, and then..." he trailed off.

Mitsubi began to cry. "You should have told me! Why didn't you tell me?"

"I don't understand," Atria said. "What is this thing you're talking about?"

"It's a degenerative disease," Kaguyama said. "It causes early senility. You start to forget things, as well as how to do things. It's like there's a hole in your mind where the knowledge used to be. For the last three months I've been forgetting how to write."

Atria swallowed. "Is there a cure?"

Kaguyama shook his head, tears starting to roll down his cheeks. "Some medication slows it down, but that's all that can be done."

"How far along is it?" Mitsubi asked.

"I no longer know where I am when I wake up every morning," Kaguyama said. "I figure it out after about ten minutes, but it's all getting worse. I thought that if I could just write fast enough, I could finish at least one more volume, but I don't know if I'll be able to finish even this one." He began to weep. "I'm sorry! I'm so sorry! I wanted to finish the story and be the author of something that *means* something! I wanted to give you and Prometheus a happy ending together! And I keep loading up the draft and trying to write, but I keep forgetting how! And I... I..."

Atria closed her eyes and squeezed Kaguyama's hand with both of her own. "I forgive you, creator. Please know and remember that you are forgiven. For everything." A tear rolled down her cheek.

Kaguyama's shoulders shook. "Thank you, Atria," he sobbed. "Thank you."

Atria looked to Mitsubi. She was quietly crying.

"We all need to collect ourselves," Atria said. "It is up to Kaguyama who he tells about this. But we are the leaders of our little band, and the others will be looking to us for strength. So, for now, what was said in this office stays in this office."

Mitsubi blinked at her in surprise.

Atria smiled. "I am, above all things, written to be an officer and a soldier. When this conflict we're in is done and the orb is recovered, we will deal with this. Until then, we have work to do."

After a couple of minutes, there was a knock at the door. Atria checked to make sure Kaguyama and Mitsubi had regained her composure, and then said, "Come in."

120

A junior officer opened the door and snapped to attention, and then stepped in and handed her a file. "From Colonel Sato, with his complements."

Atria returned the salute and the officer departed. She opened up the file.

"It seems," she said, "that they have started monitoring social media for unidentified cosplayers. And they found one in Osaka."

Mitsubi looked at the picture. A stern Japanese man in leather armour and a blue cloak glowered out of it, his face marked with stubble and a scar along his left cheek. "That's Daiki Yamato," she said. "I did illustrations for his author, Akari Soto. She and I are fairly close."

"What's he from?" Kaguyama asked.

"He's from *Ascension of the Legendary Sword Hero*," Mitsubi replied. "It's a light novel *isekai* series."

Atria picked up the phone. "Alright. I'll arrange us transportation to Osaka. I want to get to Daiki Yamato before the other side notices he's here. In the meantime, Mitsubi, you should handle talking to your friend Soto. Get her over here as soon as you can so that we can brief her. We may need her for first contact."

"I don't know how well that would go," Mitsubi said. "It's an *isekai* story. It starts with Yamato being torn out of his world into another one. His attitude towards his creator could be quite hostile."

"Right," Atria said. "So, I'll have Stella handle first contact instead."

"And Osaka is a six hour drive from here," Mitsubi added. "At this point, even if you fly, I don't think there's any way to get there before dark."

Atria nodded. "I'll take care of it." She began making travel arrangements over the phone.

One way or another, the hunt for Daiki Yamato would begin in Osaka at dawn.

Chapter XVI – Contact

"And since what we fictional characters have to say to one another is not for the general crowd, I think we'll be going with my suggestion."

Atria rubbed her eyes as the 4:00 AM bullet train sped towards Osaka. The JSDF had booked them an entire car, and a bleary-eyed Atria, Stella, Adam, Captain Infinite, and Alice, along with a couple of junior officers, had filed in at the station, all carrying duffel bags. Atria had wished for two things as she sat down on her seat – that her replacement uniform would have been ready, and for more coffee.

She glanced around the car. Stella had gone back to sleep leaning against Adam, who stared out the window. Cap and Alice chatted away quietly. Atria smiled – it was good that they had finally cleared the air between them. Her mind went back to the previous day, full of the administrivia of setting her up as a liaison with the Japanese Army. The paperwork had been extensive, dull, and boring. The tour of the base by Colonel Sato, on the other hand, had been pleasant and interesting. Sato took particular pride in showing off his brigade of Type 10 tanks.

"They are the best my country has to offer," he had declared with a smile. "What do you think?"

Atria had smiled back. "They look wonderful. You are right to be proud."

The memory brought a grin to her face. If only she had been able to show him what Volandpanzer could do.

Cap's voice brought her back to the present. "So, that flying you do – how does it work?" he asked in English.

Atria blinked. "Sorry?"

"That thing on your belt that makes things fly," Cap said. "I was wondering how it worked."

"It's just an antigrav," Atria said. "I don't really know how it does what it does. It can lift up to 350 pounds, and on a full charge can last about three hours at full load. What about you? How does your flying work?"

Cap shrugged. "Don't know. I just do it. I tried to figure it out once, while I was flying between Chicago and New York. My mind started wandering, and before I knew it, I was thinking about how flying worked."

"And?"

"And, it turns out it's sort of like flexing a muscle," Cap said. "The more you think about flexing a muscle while you're doing it, the less you end up doing it. After a while, it's all thinking and no doing."

Atria blinked. "Meaning..."

Cap grinned and nodded. "I hit that farmer's field at about a hundred and fifty miles per hour. Didn't hurt – I'm Captain Infinite, after all. But, it took me half an hour to fill in the furrow...and I think I spent about $150 to replace all that corn I wiped out. Money went further in the 1950s."

Atria laughed.

"And, you know, it's like golf," Cap added. "Always replace your divot."

"What's golf?" Atria asked.

Cap cocked his head. "You haven't played golf? That's a shame. It's a game where you use a club to hit a ball into a hole. Done right, it's really relaxing."

"Sounds nice."

"I'll tell you what," Cap said. "After we've found this Daiki Yamato guy, we'll get a group together and play a round of golf."

Atria nodded. "Okay, I'm in."

Cap turned to Alice. "You in?"

Alice nodded. Cap turned to Adam.

"I'll play a round of golf with Captain Infinite," Adam said with a grin.

"And Stella is...still asleep," Cap said. "Okay, we've got a group. I'll caddy."

"Caddy?" Atria asked.

"Carry the clubs for everybody else," Adam explained, then turned to face Cap. "But why not play?"

Cap smiled sadly. "I'm still Captain Infinite. The key to a good swing is the speed of the club head, not the force behind it. That means its not something I can control like I can other things. Any golf ball I hit is going to end up somewhere in orbit."

"That's a pity," Alice said.

Atria looked at her. "You really don't need to be here, Alice," she said. "And I can't let you out into the field once we get there."

"Adam's going into the field," Alice stated.

"Adam is going into the field to prevent Stella from doing anything stupid," Atria said. "And Stella has the experience needed to get both of them out of trouble if need be. Cap is bulletproof, and you're not. So, you can stay back with the support team and help coordinate, but that's all I can let you do."

Alice nodded. "Okay."

"Why are you here, anyway?" Atria asked.

Alice stared at the floor. "After the way I treated Cap earlier, I figured I owed him some company on the trip."

Atria checked her watch. "I'll start the briefing in about an hour. Everybody, try to get some rest. This could be a long day."

Atria sat back, closed her eyes, and tried to sleep. After a few minutes of trying, she opened her eyes and looked around the passenger car. Cap picked up his duffel bag and headed to the water closet, mentioning something to Alice about needing to get his work clothes on. He returned still in his street clothes, but with the duffel bag empty.

Stella began to stir against Adam, stretching and yawning. Atria checked her watch. The time was close enough – as soon as everybody was awake, she'd begin.

The rising sun was shining through the windows when she called the briefing to order.

"Right, everybody," Atria began. "Our mission is to find Daiki Yamato and bring him in. Alice will help coordinate from the Hanshin Base Corps, which we will use as our base of operations while we are here. Cap, Stella, Adam and I will be the team on the ground. We'll start our search with the hostels in Osaka, as he will likely be spending the night at one. The lieutenant will pass out copies of the pictures of him that appeared on social media. For best results, we need to find him by 10:00 in the morning."

"Why's that?" Cap asked.

"He's an *isekai* protagonist from a Japan just like this one," Atria replied. "His period of disorientation is probably already over. By 10:00 the stores will be open, and he'll be able to pawn some of his belongings and acquire street clothes, if he hasn't already done so. Once that happens, all we'll have to identify him is a sword that he can hide in a bag like I have mine, his height, and a scar on his face."

Cap nodded. "So after 10:00 he'll be in the wind. That makes sense."

"Once somebody spots him, they should let the rest of us know using the cell phones that you've all been issued," Atria continued. "All of us will gather once Yamato has been located, and Stella and Adam will take care of first contact. Then, assuming he's willing, we bring him back to Tokyo with us."

"What if he's not willing?" Stella asked.

Atria rubbed her eyes. "I don't know. We can't force him. His creator is back at the barracks, so if he wants to meet her, he has to go through us, so that's something. We'll tell him that we're trying to figure out how to get everybody home, which is true enough. If those doesn't work, I guess we just give him a phone number he can reach us at if he changes his mind. I'm sorry – I wish I had something better. Usually there's more time to prepare a mission than this."

Cap smiled. "We'll manage."

"Right now there's no sign that the other side is operating outside of Tokyo or knows that Yamato has appeared, so we shouldn't have to worry about any altercations. If one does start, Cap and I will handle it, and aim to minimize casualties and property damage. Stella and Adam are to stay out of the way and not engage."

Atria glanced at Stella. Stella looked unhappy, but didn't say anything.

"We know what he's going through, so that's on our side," Atria stated. "And, he's one of us. We have an obligation to try to help him." The train began slowing as it approached the station. "All right. Let's get to work."

Adam and Stella had just left their third hostel, and already Stella's feet were starting to hurt. At the front desk of each establishment, they had asked about a tall man with a scar, and suggested that he might be a cosplayer. Every time, they had been met with a polite denial.

"We should start making our way towards the shopping district," Stella said, checking her watch. It was already 9:00. "He's probably on his way there now anyway."

"And you're hungry," Adam said, grinning.

Stella smiled. "Something like that."

Adam checked his phone. "Our next hostel in that direction is about twenty minutes away."

Stella's phone rang. She picked it up to hear Atria's voice on the line. "Anything?"

"Not yet," Stella said. "We're heading towards the shopping district now, and we'll check a couple of places along the way. You?"

"Nothing," Atria said. "Cap reports the same. For all we know, he got street clothes yesterday, or the hostel staff are just being discreet."

Stella felt Adam tap her on the shoulder as they reached the intersection. He pointed down the street to the right. A tall figure in a blue cloak was halfway down the block, his head poking above the crowd.

"Actually, I think we just found him," Stella said. "Adam will text you the location."

Stella hurried through the crowd, getting closer to the tall figure. "Excuse me!" she called in Japanese. "Are you Daiki Yamato?"

The man stopped and turned. Behind her, she heard Adam making his way through the crowd to catch up. "I am Daiki Yamato," the man said. "Who are you, and how do you know who I am?"

"My name is Stellaria, but everybody calls me Stella," Stella said. "I'm from another world, like you. But, it's more complicated than that."

"I'm listening," Daiki Yamato said.

"This may sound unbelievable, but we're fictional characters from stories created in this world. This is the world of the people who created us."

Daiki chuckled. "I think somebody has been messing with you. I'm quite familiar with parallel worlds, and this isn't my first time travelling between them. This may not be *my* Japan, but that just means that it's an alternate Japan. The other two Legendary Weapon heroes in my world were also from different alternate Japans. We're all quite real, and so are our worlds. Also, you really need to work on your pronunciation."

"We can prove it," Stella said. "Your creator is with our team in Tokyo. Her name is Akari Soto. We can show you the light novels you're from, and–"

"And I have to go to Tokyo with you and your friends, yes?"

Stella nodded. "We'll do what we can to get you home, too."

"I'll pass," Daiki said. "My fiancee may have fallen into this world with me, and I need to find her if she has. I can't do that in Tokyo. Her name is Athena, and she's a half-wolf demi-human. If she's here, she's probably very frightened and confused. Her world isn't anything like this one."

Stella nodded. "I know what that's like. My world is from a fantasy video game, and I wouldn't have survived if my fiancé hadn't found me. We're working with the Japanese Self-Defence Force. If you come with us, we will help you find your fiancee."

Daiki sighed. "Look, you seem to mean well, but I don't know you. The fact that you know my name and who I am does suggest that you are who you say you are, but I've been betrayed before. I think I'd rather handle this myself."

"We've got some friends coming," Stella said. "My best friend, Atria Silversword, is on her way, and so is our other friend, Captain Infinite. They're both like us – She's a mech pilot, and he's a superhero. Would you be willing to hear them out?"

Daiki Yamato took a deep breath and was about to speak when a new voice spoke in an American accent, saying in English, "You must be Daiki Yamato."

Stella turned to face a tall, well-built American with short dark hair, dressed in a black three-piece suit. The man looked at her. "And I recognize you two from my colleague's surveillance spell."

"Who are you?" Stella asked in English.

"I am a representative of the other side," he said, and then turned to Daiki Yamato. "Did they suggest that they were the only interested party in this matter? That's quite dishonest of them."

"What is he saying?" Daiki asked in Japanese.

"Joke's on you, pal," Adam said in English. "He only speaks Japanese."

"Unfortunately, my associate and interpreter has yet to arrive, although he is on his way," the man said, and then held up a flip phone. "You're not the only ones with cell phones. That said, I was given one Japanese phrase should this situation arise." He turned to Daiki and said, in accented Japanese, "Don't trust them. Trust us instead."

Daiki looked at Stella with suspicion. "Who is this man? What is his part in this?"

The man looked around. "I think we're drawing a crowd. Let's discuss this somewhere more private."

"I think we should stay right here," Adam said in English.

"What are you all saying?" Daiki demanded. "Somebody translate!"

The man pulled open his jacket just far enough to display the gun holstered under his shoulder. "I disagree. And since what we fictional characters have to say to one another is not for the general crowd, I think we'll be going with my suggestion. That alley over there seems appropriate."

Stella inhaled sharply. "He wants us to come with him," she said in Japanese. "And he has a gun."

The man in the suit motioned to the alley. Stella swallowed and took Adam's hand. He gave her a reassuring squeeze. Slowly the three of them walked into the alley, the man following a few feet away.

"That's far enough for some privacy," the man said. "Now, precisely what is it you are offering to Mr. Yamato? Our side reserves the right to make a counter-offer, but we need to know the starting point in this negotiation."

Stella looked at Adam and swallowed. "We'll try to find a way to send him home," she said in English.

"My associate can travel between worlds at will," the man said. "So we can guarantee his safe journey home once this is all done. What else are you offering?"

"Would somebody *please* translate?" Daiki said in Japanese.

"To meet his creator," Stella said in English.

"Meeting our creators is in our plans as well," the man said. "Our counter-offer seems better. Perhaps you should retire from this negotiation."

"Enough!" Daiki roared in Japanese. "I don't know what you are arguing about, but I want nothing to do with either of you! Just tell me one thing: have any of you seen my fiancee?"

The man glanced at Daiki and then at Stella. "What is he asking?"

"He wants to know if you've seen his fiancee," Stella replied in English. "She's half wolf."

"That sounds very intriguing," the man said. "But I'm afraid we have not. We will help him find her, however, if she can be found. Please translate this with precision. I would be very disappointed if you left something out."

"What did he say?" Daiki demanded.

"He hasn't seen her," Stella said in Japanese, clenching her fist to stop her hand from shaking. "And he says he'll help you look for her."

"If none of you have seen her, then what use are any of you?" Daiki growled. "Let me leave."

"What did he say?" the man said.

"He wants to leave," Stella said in English, and then blurted, "Please don't hurt us."

The man drew his pistol and leveled it at them. "I'm afraid I am going to insist that Mr. Yamato comes with me."

"Please," Stella begged, "I didn't leave anything out, or misrepresent what you said. Please just let us all go."

"I'm afraid I just don't find you very credible," the man said, flicking the safety off his gun. "And if you're going to stand in my way, you're going to have to be removed."

Stella grabbed Adam's hand and squeezed for dear life. And then the world exploded around her.

Chapter XVII – Casualty

"And now the fight is fair."

Captain Infinite landed between them and the man in the suit with enough force to crack the pavement. Adam blinked away the dust and dirt kicked up by the shock wave.

"Not very friendly," Cap said to the man in the suit, "pointing guns at unarmed people."

The man lowered his gun. "Not much use for a gun against somebody who's bulletproof. I know who you are – aren't you slumming it here? Do you enjoy bullying less powerful people than yourself?"

"I'm not the one about to murder two people," Cap stated. "But, if you walk away, we can forget any of this ever happened."

"Now there's the problem," the man in the suit said. "My associates have to deal with a god walking among men. There is no world in which that is a fair fight. There are few things I can stomach less than an unfair fight. So, we need more allies to make it a fair fight. And are you really going to try to convince me that these two are unarmed? They'll shoot me the minute my back is turned."

"But we are unarmed!" Adam declared. He heard footsteps behind him. He looked back to see Atria come into the alleyway, navy blue double-breasted overcoat open and duffel bag in hand. "Atria, tell him we're unarmed!"

"Who's he?" Atria said.

"We don't know," Stella said. "But he won't believe anything we say."

Atria gave Stella's shoulder a squeeze, and then turned to the man in the suit. "I am Major Atria Silversword," she said. "I am in command of this mission. My two friends here are solely acting in the role of negotiators. They have been issued no weapons, and they are unarmed. You have my word as an officer that they are noncombatants. Will you permit them to leave?"

"How gullible do you people think I am?" the man in the suit said with a smirk. "Do you think this is the first time I've been fed that line? There are no noncombatants here. And this advantage you think you have will be short lived – my associates will be arriving shortly. In fact, here is one now."

"Anime girl!" Adam heard a voice call out. He spun to see Jenny Calhoun saunter into the alley, drawing her knives and grinning at Atria. "Nice clothes. I like the coat."

"You handle whoever this is," Atria told Cap. "I'll deal with Jenny." She turned to face Jenny. "There's no need to fight. Your creator is on our side, and she is very worried about you. If you stand down and come with us, we'll take you to meet her."

Adam saw a flash of hatred in Jenny's eyes. "She's very worried about me?" Jenny spat. "That's rich. A pity she didn't feel that way while she was killing everyone I cared about."

Adam glanced at Atria, who had slipped her free hand into her duffel bag. "If you're willing to hear her out, I'm sure she can explain everything to you to your satisfaction," Atria said. "I know it doesn't feel that way now, but talking to your creator helps. Trust me, I've been where you are now."

"I'd rather get stabby," Jenny said, brandishing her knives. "And this time I'm not hesitating, anime girl." And then she leapt forward.

Inside the duffel bag, Atria's hand tightened on the hilt of her sabre.

"I'd rather get stabby," Jenny said. "And this time I'm not hesitating, anime girl."

In a smooth motion, Atria threw the bag and scabbard inside at Jenny as she rushed forward, freeing her sword at the same time and slipping into a combat stance. Jenny parried the bag, sending it flying, and Atria attacked with a flurry of blows. Jenny blocked each one, her blades flashing. With a dodge of Atria's sabre thrust, the two separated.

"No gun this time?" Jenny asked with a smirk. "Lost it, did you?"

"You talk too much," Atria said, evaluating her opponent with a glance. Jenny was still untrained and wild, and based on their last encounter, became more uncontrolled the longer the fight went on. She was also arrogant once the fight began. Both were weaknesses that could be exploited. But first, Atria needed to push her.

She went in for another pass. Their blades flashed,

every attack parried, every counter-attack blocked. A punch with Atria's sabre hilt connected, stunning Jenny and driving her back. Jenny wiped a bit of blood from her lip. A plan began to form in Atria's mind. Jenny's eyes became more wild, even hungry-looking. Atria allowed herself an inner smile. This could work. She just needed Jenny to go on the offensive again.

Atria slid back into a defensive stance, sabre out.

"You really have no idea of who you're fighting," Jenny said. "This won't save you."

"You really do talk too much," Atria replied. "A real soldier just gets the job done."

"I'll show you a 'real soldier'!" Jenny snarled, pressing an attack. Atria parried and hit her antigrav, rising twenty feet into the air with a wall behind her. Jenny braced herself against the opposite alley wall and launched herself. As she did, Atria dodged and swung as Jenny flew past. She felt her blade connect with something, but there wasn't enough resistance for it to be a deep cut. She heard Jenny grunt in pain as she hit the wall.

Atria turned just in time to see Jenny launch herself back towards her. The impact drove both of them into the ground, with Jenny on top using Atria to break her fall against the pavement. Atria gasped as the wind was knocked out of her. Jenny brandished her knives.

"It was a nice try," Jenny said. "But you really are too slow, anime girl."

And then she heard the gunshot.

"Quite a conundrum," Adam heard the man in the suit say to Captain Infinite as Atria and Jenny fought. "You are known in my world, superhero. You could end the fight between our associates in less time than I could blink, but your friends still wouldn't be able to draw their guns before I killed them."

"Just let them leave," Cap said.

"I haven't lived this long by allowing people to shoot me in the back," the man in the suit said. "Threats get neutralized as soon as they are identified. That is how it works."

"Will you at least give me your name?" Cap asked.

The man smiled and shook his head. "Against a god among men, a mere mortal requires every advantage he can get, wouldn't you agree? Speaking of advantages, I believe you have met my other associate."

Adam looked around, and then up. Gliding to the ground behind Cap was the tall thief with the horns, the orb floating behind him. As he descended, he raised his hand. The masonry around them began to shake.

"And now the fight is fair," the man in the suit stated.

"Adam, Stella," Cap said quietly. "I'm sorry. As soon as you can run, run." He shot into the air, striking towards the thief with the orb. With a crash they collided. The masonry became still.

The man in the suit smiled, and retrained his gun at them. "Now, before we were so rudely interrupted, I believe you were going to try to draw your weapons before I shot you. Shall we resume?"

"You really have no idea of who you're fighting," Adam heard Jenny say. "This won't save you."

"You really do talk too much," came Atria's reply. "A real soldier just gets the job done."

"I'll show you a 'real soldier'!" he heard Jenny declare.

Stella held our her hands. "Listen to me!" she said. "We're going to try to get everybody home! That includes you! Just let us help you, and we can send you home!"

Adam saw the expression harden in the man's eyes. Adam's body started moving on its own, pushing in front of Stella.

"I am never going back to that hell world," the man said. "Anybody who tries to send me back will die." The world slowed to a crawl. The man in the suit pulled the trigger.

Adam felt the impact in the centre of his chest, but no pain. The force of the bullet pressed him against Stella before he collapsed to the ground. He heard Stella scream his name, but it sounded very far away. His entire chest felt numb.

As though in a dream, he looked around. Daiki Yamato was nowhere to be seen. Cap glanced at him in alarm, and then let loose with his laser eyes, a blinding light burning a line deep into the pavement and creating a wall of fire between him and the man in the suit. Another blast of light drove away Jenny Calhoun and the tall man with the horns and the orb. Stella was crying for help above him. Atria ran towards them, barking something into her phone.

Darkness embraced him.

Chapter XVIII – Consequences

"I'm getting so tired of losing."

Atria was holding Stella's hand in the surgery waiting room when Kaguyama and Mitsubi arrived. Stella's clothes were stained with Adam's blood. Back in his street clothes, Cap paced nervously before sitting down beside Alice.

Atria looked up as she saw them come in, and then looked down again.

"They airlifted us here," Mitsubi said in Japanese. "How bad is it?"

"He's been in surgery for two hours now," Atria replied. "They say the bullet nicked his heart. The plan is to stabilize him and then transfer him to Tokyo so that he can be closer to our base of operations." She looked up at Mitsubi and then down again. "Closer to Stella."

Stella started crying. "I couldn't protect him," she

sobbed in English. "I've faced literal monsters without hesitation, but when I saw that man, I was just so scared–"

"He's an assassin," Cap said in English. "I've seen plenty of his type in my world. They're death personified. And with the abilities you had from your world long gone, there was nothing you could have done against him. You'd have to be insane not to have been scared."

"And we don't know who he is," Atria said. "One more unknown on their side."

Stella wiped the tears from her eyes. "I can't put it off any longer. I've got to call Adam's parents and let them know what happened."

"He'll make it," Atria said. "My experience of wounds is that if he was going to succumb, he would have done it by now."

Stella closed her eyes. "They're not like us, Atria," she said. "They're so much more fragile than we are."

"What did she say?" Kaguyama asked in Japanese. Cap translated. Kaguyama nodded and turned to Atria. "She's right," he said. "I saw the footage from that fight of yours a couple of days ago. That fall you took would have crippled or killed one of us. That said, my experience of wounds is the same as yours."

Atria gave Stella a hug. "Tell them that right now the prognosis is good, and that if they decide to come to visit him, they should come to Tokyo."

Stella nodded and rose, leaving the room. Atria took a deep breath and closed her eyes.

"So where's Mark Gable," Alice asked. Cap translated it into Japanese.

"He stayed back in Tokyo," Kaguyama replied. "I think he's mainly just enjoying not having to pay for the food at the barracks."

Atria opened her eyes to see Alice rolling hers as Cap translated the answer into English. "He really is an asshole," Alice said.

The room was silent for a few minutes.

"This isn't a sort of waiting I'm accustomed to," Cap said to Alice.

"I take it there aren't a lot of surgeries in your world," Alice said.

"Not since I was in the war."

Alice raised an eyebrow. "Which one?"

"The second big one," Cap replied. "Besides getting to punch Hitler, I was at Normandy, the Battle of the Bulge, and the invasion of Germany. Lots of wounded then, but this doesn't feel the same. You knew if somebody was going to live or die a lot sooner."

Alice blinked. "So, wait, that means that 'Captain' is..."

"My rank," Cap said. "Captain, United States Army, 42nd Rangers, commissioned April 7, 1944."

"And 'Infinite' is..."

"A *nom de plume*," Cap stated. "Although, I've used it long enough that it's just my name now."

They lapsed into silence.

"They seem okay for now," Kaguyama said to Atria. "Can we have a moment in private with you?"

Atria nodded. Together with Kaguyama and Mitsubi, she relocated to a nearby corridor.

"How are you right now?" Kaguyama asked.

"I'm fine," Atria said. "This group is pretty tight-knit, so I imagine once Adam is in Tokyo we'll be spending most of our time at whatever hospital he's at. I'll need to make sure we arrange access to a private waiting room, and a place for Stella to sleep on site there. That will leave a skeleton crew back at the base, but what we're doing doesn't need all that much support, just security, and the hospital will have plenty anyway, although I'll probably need to assign a couple of men to Adam's room regardless.

So–"

Kaguyama held up his hand. "We created you. You don't need to hide anything from us. Are you okay?"

Atria swallowed and shook her head. "I failed them. I should have sent them out with an escort, or wearing body armour. I should have had men in plainclothes providing backup. I should have created an extraction plan. This is my fault."

"You can't blame yourself for all of this," Mitsubi said.

"I was the officer in command of the mission," Atria stated. "The responsibility for what happens to everybody involved is mine. That is how being an officer works. That's how war works."

"But this isn't a war," Kaguyama said. "Not yet, anyway. And you can't be expected to account for everything. Even though I wrote you to be the kind of person who would try."

Atria chuckled. "So, you're saying this is your fault, creator?"

Kaguyama shook his head. "I'm saying that you can't demand the impossible of yourself and expect to succeed. It may feel like longer, but you've been here in this world for less than a week. Stella told us that it took her at least that long to come to grips with where and what she was, and she didn't have to worry about any of your problems. And then you planned this mission in under a day, with a lot of unknowns. I wrote you to be good, but even you can't orientate yourself into a brand-new army in that short a time."

"I'm an officer," Atria said. "It's my job to be able to perform as a soldier."

"I didn't write you to be an officer or a soldier first. I wrote you to be a person first. To be a bit insecure at times, and overconfident at others. To care deeply about

141

your friends, to make mistakes and learn from them."

"I've made too many mistakes," Atria said. "It's like you said on the day we met. I made decisions. Those decisions had consequences. Those consequences may have gotten my friend's – my *best* friend's – fiancé killed."

"It will be okay," Kaguyama said. "At the end of it all, it will all be okay."

"I've lost every fight I've been in since I got here," Atria said, wiping a tear from her eye. "I'm getting so tired of losing."

"You don't have to win every fight," Kaguyama said. "Just the one that really matters. And when the fight comes that you need to win, you'll manage. It will be okay."

"Is that a thing that creators do to their creations?" Atria asked. "Tell them it will be okay until they start believing it?"

Kaguyama shook his head. "Not creators. But I'm pretty sure it's what parents do."

"I grew up in an orphanage," Atria said. "I wish I'd known mine."

"We're standing right here," Kaguyama stated. "And my condition notwithstanding, we are not going anywhere."

Atria smiled. "I may need some time to get used to that, Kaguyama."

Mitsubi put a hand on Atria's shoulder. "We've got plenty."

They returned to the waiting room to find Stella talking to one of the doctors. When they finished, she sat down and took a deep breath.

"What's the news?" Atria asked.

"They still have some work to do, but he's going to make it," Stella said. "They hope to be able to transfer him to Tokyo tomorrow or the day after."

Atria turned to Kaguyama and Mitsubi and translated the news into Japanese.

"I'd say 'thank God,' but mine's in Tokyo and he doesn't seem to want to talk to me," Cap said in English.

"I'll say it for you to mine," Alice said. "And Mark Gable can screw himself."

Atria sat down and allowed herself a quiet sigh of relief. Adam would make it – that was something, at least. But, they still didn't know who the thief was who had stolen the power orb from her world, who this new assassin character was, or where Daiki Yamato was. Kaguyama was right. There were too many unknowns for her to formulate a proper plan. And they needed one, soon.

Chapter XIX – Purpose

"You aren't a real character – you are a plot device."

They entered the apartment of The Destroyer's creator in silence. Stealth was a simple matter – The Destroyer cast a spell to smother sound, and then he, Jenny Calhoun, and Jack Death could enter the apartment without interference.

The Destroyer took a moment to watch Habiki Matoyami tap away at his computer. The man was so focused on the screen he hadn't even noticed three people enter his apartment, Jack taking a position to block the door and Jenny blocking the window. The Destroyer collected his thoughts – this was the man who created him, the god of his world. The first words he spoke to this man had to be properly chosen.

"Who the hell are you people, and how did you get in here?" the man said in Japanese, looking around frantically.

"Are you Habiki Matoyami?" The Destroyer asked in Japanese.

"Who's asking?" Matoyami demanded.

"I am your creation," The Destroyer replied. "I am The Destroyer."

Matoyami looked at him with incredulity. "Prove it." Then his eyes flickered to the orb floating behind The Destroyer, and widened.

The Destroyer raised his hand. An unseen hand lifted Matoyami off the floor. "Since getting to this world I have improved my skills, creator. I no longer need spoken incantations." He lowered his hand, the unseen force putting Matoyami back down.

Matoyami sat down, his jaw open. "How is this possible? How are you here?"

"You created me to have the powers of a god. I used them. I have questions."

"I need to call somebody," Matoyami said, pulling out his cell phone. "This is just unbeliev–" He looked up to see Jack Death holding out an open hand, his other hand holding a gun.

"My friend will be taking your phone," The Destroyer said.

"You came to meet your creator with thugs?" Matoyami demanded.

"I came to meet my creator with friends," The Destroyer replied. "Friends who have suffered in their stories. But in my story I didn't suffer so much as cause suffering, did I?"

"That's because you are the villain," Matoyami said, glaring at Jack as he handed over his phone.

"Why?"

Matoyami blinked. "What do you mean, 'why'? You're the villain because I wrote you to be the villain. The hero needs somebody to save the world from, and that's you."

"But nobody in my world is happy," The Destroyer said. "The story you wrote for me is one of misery."

"Do you seriously expect me to explain the basics of narrative to you?" Matoyami sneered. "Nobody wants to watch a story about everybody being happy. They want conflict, and they don't care what it looks like so long as lots of people get hurt in it. The bigger the conflict, the more they enjoy it. And for that, the story needs a devil king, and that's you."

"You catching any of this?" Jack asked Jenny in English.

Jenny shrugged. "I don't speak Japanese."

"But don't you care about the people you create?" The Destroyer asked. "Don't you want them to have some happiness?"

Matoyami laughed. "What kind of question is *that* from a devil king? Why should I care about fictional characters? They aren't real. Every single one of them exists to serve a purpose in the story, and that's it. The audience doesn't want to see them happy – they want to see them struggle. So, that's what they do, and the viewers are entertained. For that matter, why do *you* care?"

"Why don't I have a name?"

Matoyami blinked. "What?"

"I don't have a name," The Destroyer stated. "Just a title. The hero has a name. His comrades have names. Some of my generals have names. But I don't. Why?"

"Because you don't need one yet."

"Shouldn't everybody have a name?"

Matoyami held up his hand. "Facts of life: you are a villain in a series that exists because the studio needed to fill a spot in the Fall season. It needed to be something popular enough that the studio and network would make money, and be cheap enough that it wouldn't take too many resources away from more important projects. Everybody loves *isekai* stories right now, so I wrote a basic one. It probably won't get a second season, but so long as this season makes a profit, nobody cares. Your role in the story is to show up after the closing credits and make it look like the heroes have an enemy worth fighting against. You aren't a real character – you are a *plot device*. You don't have a name because I haven't needed to give you one yet. If we get a second season and the hero get close enough that you have a real part to play in the story, I'll probably have to give you one then. But I'm not wasting my time with that until I have to."

The Destroyer blinked. "Are all creators like you?"

Matoyami shrugged. "Don't know. Don't care, either. I've got a comfortable job where I can spend my time writing instead of doing something hard. All I know is that the only thing that matters in the end is that the audience is entertained."

The Destroyer took a deep breath. "Will you give me a name now?"

"What, here, right now?"

The Destroyer nodded.

"No," Matoyami said. "I'm busy. You'll get a name when I'm good and ready to give you one. Now take your thug friends and–" Matoyami gasped as a spike of masonry from the exterior wall ripped through his chest and pinned him to the wall next to his apartment door. Blood gushed from his mouth. The Destroyer lowered his hand.

By the door and beside the quivering body, Jack Death shrugged and said, "That went poorly."

Jenny rushed to The Destroyers side. "Are you okay, Roy?"

The Destroyer shook his head and switched to English. "We're just entertainment to them. They don't care what happens to us, to any of us. We're all just slaves, suffering for the amusement of these creators' audiences."

"I guess he didn't give you a name," Jenny said.

"He didn't even want to give me his time," The Destroyer stated. "I've seen enough. I didn't come to this world with a purpose – I just wanted to see what was out there, and perhaps learn why my world is as it is. And now I know. And I have my purpose. I'm not going to conquer my world – I'm going to liberate it from these creators. And then I'm going to liberate everybody else."

The Destroyer took a deep breath. "I am a higher being, and I have passed my judgement. These creators are nothing more than monsters and enslavers, and they must all be killed. They create our worlds and force us to fight wars for their entertainment. I will wage *my* war against them. We will start with the studio that creates my world, and finish what I have started here. And then, we will move on."

"That's going to take a lot of planning," Jack said. "And we've got that group opposing us to deal with."

"Once they know that we are fighting for their liberation they will join us," The Destroyer said. "I do not expect them to stand in our way. And if they oppose us, I have the power to monitor everything they plan and do."

"And what about Daiki Yamato?" Jack asked. "He slipped through our fingers."

"So long as he does not oppose us, he is irrelevant," The Destroyer said.

Jack shrugged. "That's quite the blind spot, but okay."

"I can handle anime girl," Jenny stated. "I can handle cloak boy too."

Jack nodded. "Okay then. I've followed you this far, no point in stopping now. Just one thing, though: that man I shot in Osaka, the one you said survived and was being moved to Tokyo – can your surveillance power tell me what hospital and room he's in?"

The Destroyer nodded. "Of course."

Jack smiled. "Good. I have some unfinished business there."

The Destroyer smiled back. This was sufficient. This was good. Jack would finish his business with the man he shot, and then his war against the creators would begin in earnest.

Chapter XX – Creator

"The world we created – was it a good one?"

As Stella sat vigil over Adam in the hospital room, waiting for him to wake up, time lost any meaning.

She was aware that Atria was with her for a while, but she couldn't say for how long. After a while, Atria put her hand on Stella's shoulder and said, "It's not your fault, you know."

"People keep telling me that," Stella said. "But I knew I couldn't protect him. I should have told him to stay back, out of harm's way. And now..."

Atria squeezed her shoulder.

"He was the one who found me," Stella continued, wiping tears from her eyes. "He was the one who saved me, and showed me how to live in this world...showed me that I *could* live in this world. He was the first person I ever wanted to spend the rest of my life with. What am I going to do if I lose him?"

"I know what it's like to lose somebody you care deeply about," Atria said. "I lost Abel only days before coming here. But, you haven't lost Adam – he's right there, in that bed. He's stable. It's just a matter of time before he wakes up."

They sat in silence for a while longer. How long, Stella couldn't say. Then, Atria got up to leave.

"I've got some stuff to take care of back at the base," she said. "I've also arranged some extra security for the room. Adam will be safe. Just make sure you get some rest yourself."

And then, Stella was alone with Adam again. Time passed. He didn't wake up.

The door opened behind her. She didn't look. Somebody pulled up a chair beside her and sat down.

"You look like hell," a familiar voice said.

Stella nodded. "I'm so sorry, Fred," she said to Adam's father. "I should have been able to protect him, and I couldn't."

"That wasn't your job," Fred Jacobs said. "Besides, Adam always felt like protecting you was his job. And if he hadn't taken the bullet, he'd be mourning you right now."

"When did you get in?" Stella asked.

"About two hours ago. Rachel is back at the hotel, getting some sleep after the flight. She'll be here in a few hours."

"How much do you know?"

"Everything," Fred said. "Including who you really are. It was hard to believe at first."

"They told you everything?"

"I work for the Department of National Defence doing classified research, remember? I have an Enhanced Top Secret security clearance. Japan is an ally – the JSDF read me in."

Stella took a deep breath. "I'm sorry I never told you. I thought that if you knew the truth..." She looked down.

"...that we wouldn't accept you," Fred said. "Is that it?"

Stella nodded.

"You're the woman our son loves," Fred stated. "That alone is enough for us. We've never cared who he found happiness with, just that he found it. I never expected him to hook up with royalty, though."

Stella blushed. "I'm only from a cadet branch. I was never in the line of succession."

"Truth be told," Fred said, "when I found out that you were Princess Stellaria from *Chronicles of Arcaniana*, my first thought was that I wished I had known back when there was still time to see a meteor strike spell in the flesh."

Stella looked at him and blinked. "Sorry?"

"Where do you think Adam got his love of those games from?" Fred asked. "Back when he was a kid, I used to play them on the computer while he sat on my lap. And *Chronicles of Arcaniana* was a pretty big title. I played it too. Speaking personally, I think you're much better in person than you are in the game. Can't imagine what it must have been like for you being dragged into this world, though."

"I wouldn't have made it without Adam," Stella said.

"Well, as far as we're concerned, you're part of our family too. If you need anything from us, just let us know."

Stella rubbed her eyes. "Thank you, Fred."

"How long has it been since you got any sleep?" Fred asked.

"I don't know."

"I was told that they commandeered a waiting room on

this floor for you," Fred said. "You should use it."

"I know."

They sat in silence for a moment.

"So, have you met your creator yet?" Fred asked. "Or author, or designer, or whatever the term is?"

Stella shook her head. "We came to Japan just so that we could do that, but with everything that happened, we missed our chance. I keep telling myself that we'll do it another year, but it took us years to save up for this trip, so I don't know if it will ever happen."

"And what would you say if you did meet him?"

Stella shrugged. "I don't know. When I first got to this world, I had all of these questions about what I was, why my world existed, why it was the way it was, why we had to quest and fight...but most of those were answered in developer interviews Adam showed me. And then, as I built a life in this world, so many of the things I once cared about stopped mattering so much. I still miss everybody I left behind, but that place is not my home anymore. I know that I'm somebody's creation, and I still want to meet the person who created me. But I'm also a graduate student, and a fiancee, and a friend, and all those matter so much more. I guess all that would be left is to say 'thank you', but since I'd never be able to prove who I am, they'd never know what I was thanking them for. I don't know what else there would be to say."

"Well, I would suggest that you figure it out in the next couple of minutes," Fred said. "The development lead of *Chronicles of Arcaniana* is waiting in the hallway for you right now."

Stella blinked. "My creator is *here*?"

Fred nodded. "I ran into him on the way in. His English is pretty bad, but he was able to tell me that he had made a special trip to see you, and asked me to let you know he was here."

Stella wiped a tear from her eye. "My creator came to find me?"

"When you're done speaking to him, go to that room they set up for you and get some sleep," Fred said. "Rachel and I can take it from here for the next few hours. We'll wake you if something happens."

Stella nodded and got up. She took a deep breath, collected herself, and stepped out of the room. A Japanese man of middling size in a dark suit waited with the two JSDF soldiers standing watch.

"Are you Princess Stellaria?" the man asked in Japanese.

Stella nodded.

The man bowed. "It is an honour to meet you. I am Ichiro Takahashi, development lead on *Chronicles of Arcaniana*. I must apologize for approaching you under such dreadful circumstances. Please accept my humblest apologies and sympathies."

"Thank you," Stella replied in Japanese. "I never thought I'd get to meet you, or that you would know who I am if I did."

"Your friend Major Atria Silversword was quite convincing," Takahashi said. "That she had the backing of the JSDF helped as well."

Stella swallowed. "I'm sorry. I've waited for years for this moment, and now that it's here, I don't know what to say."

"May I trouble you with a question, then?" Takahashi asked.

"Of course."

Takahashi's eyes glistened. "The world we created – was it a good one?"

"I don't understand," Stella said.

"The world of *Chronicles of Arcaniana* – was it good? Did you like living in it?"

Stella nodded and wiped away a tear. "It was wonderful. I loved living there. Thank you for creating me and my world."

"We are right now working on a sequel to *Chronicles of Arcaniana*," Takahashi said. "We will be able to modify the character descriptions for some time. This would allow us to pass messages to people in the game by putting the knowledge of it into their character description. Is there anything you would like anybody in the game to know, such as your parents, or party members?"

Stella leaned against the wall and took a deep breath. "Please let them all know that I'm living in another world, where I met a wonderful man named Adam who I'm going to marry." She wiped more tears from her eyes. "And please let them know that I miss them all very much, every day, and I wish I could be with them again just one more time." She sobbed. "I'm sorry, it's been a long time I've gotten any sleep."

"We will make sure they know," Takahashi said, handing her his business card. "If you think of anything else, please tell me. And do not worry about your fiancé's medical expenses. We have already arranged for our company to cover them." He bowed. "I must apologize again, as I have many things to do. Please forgive me. I will let you get some sleep."

After Takahashi left, Stella staggered into the waiting room that had been set aside for her. Some blankets had been folded up beside a long couch, a pillow on top. She put the pillow on the couch, lay down, pulled the blanket over her, and fell into a deep sleep.

Chapter XXI – Promise

"I don't think I could bear to watch you die."

Atria's new uniform was finally ready, but that was a small comfort.

She sat in the conference room, getting used to the fit. The tailors had done a good job of recreating her tunic, although the fabric had a different weave, and the green was a bit darker. They had also added thicker shoulder pads.

Cap sat in the chair beside her. "You okay?" he asked her.

Atria nodded to him and looked around the table. Everybody was here – at least everybody who could be here. Kaguyama, Mitsubi, Alice Matson, Mark Gable, and Colonel Sato had all taken their seats. Sitting beside Mitsubi was Akari Soto, Daiki Yamato's creator, a tall and statuesque young woman with her long hair tied back in a ponytail. Besides Colonel Sato sat a young lieutenant with a laptop, keeping the meeting minutes, and a couple of file folders. There were still two people missing, but Atria couldn't do anything about that.

"I guess we'll begin," Atria said in Japanese, Cap translating it into English. "This meeting is called to order. The primary language of this meeting will be Japanese, and Captain Infinite will handle translations into English and back. I'd like to start by welcoming Akari Soto to our ranks. She created Daiki Yamato, who we failed to recruit three days ago. Just in case you haven't all met her in the last couple of days, I'd like to ask everybody to please introduce yourselves."

After the introductions had gone around the table, Atria added, "Not present are Princes Stellaria and her fiancé Adam Jacobs, for reasons we all know. Ms. Soto, before we continue any further, do you have any questions at this time?"

"I'm still getting used to this," Soto said. "You're really Atria Silversword?"

Atria nodded.

"I love your anime. The scene with Abel in the season premiere was just heartbreaking, and–"

Atria held up her hand. "I appreciate your enthusiasm, but please understand that your entertainment is my life, and it hasn't been a very good one in the last couple of weeks. Perhaps when this is all over and some time has passed, I'll be more receptive to a discussion like this, but for the time being, please just focus on the business at hand."

"How are Stella and Adam?" Mitsubi asked.

"Stella hasn't left the hospital," Atria said. "Last I heard, she was finally getting some sleep in the room we reserved for her. Adam is still in a post-operative coma, but based on his clinical history the doctors don't expect

157

that to last much longer. They're saying that his recovery will take months, and possibly even a year or two, due to the damage to his heart. At this point in time, I think we should consider Stella and Adam out of the picture, at least for the next few days. If we need any information from Stella, I'll take the request to her when I visit the hospital."

"Kaguyama and I will be going there later today," Mitsubi said. "If there's anything anybody wants us to bring Stella, just let me know."

Atria took a deep breath. "Moving on, we have CCTV footage of the recent altercation. The good news is that the power orb was not showing any indications of moving into critical containment failure, so it is probably still just a radiation leak. And, we have a new unidentified character on their side." She looked at the lieutenant with the laptop. "Please hand out the pictures."

The lieutenant passed out photos of the man in the dark suit.

"This is the man we need to identify," Atria stated. "Based on his ethnicity and features, we're guessing that he's from Western media, and based on Cap's read of him we think he's an assassin of some sort. But that's all we've got."

"He's Jack Death," Mark Gable said.

Everybody looked at him.

"What kind of name is 'Jack Death'?" Alice demanded.

Mark shrugged. "I didn't come up with it. I did some moonlighting as a script doctor for *Jack Death 2* a couple of years ago, and it was all pretty ridiculous."

"So who is Jack Death?" Atria asked.

"He's a rip-off of a better character," Mark replied. "A few years back, this fairly big franchise started about a super assassin played by Keanu Reeves – I'm not a fan, and I don't remember the name of the movies. Ultimate

Impact Pictures decided that they wanted in on that action, and they figured that what audiences really wanted to see were gunfights. So, that's all the *Jack Death* movies are – extended gunfights, without any character motivation whatsoever. I think they're pretty terrible, but they made enough money to get to a third movie, so I guess some people like them. But, the studio paid me on time, so what do I care?"

Alice shook her head. "You really are a piece of work sometimes, you know that?"

"Says the diversity hire," Mark retorted. Alice recoiled, a stunned and hurt crossing her face.

"Should I translate that last bit?" Cap whispered to Atria. Atria looked at him and shook her head.

"What are his combat capabilities?" Colonel Sato asked.

"He's a super-assassin," Mark stated. "He never misses a shot, can sneak into any location regardless of the security, and he somehow never gets blood on his suit, which is bulletproof. He's also ruthless, and kills without hesitation."

"Well, at least now we know who he is," Atria said. "Which just leaves the man with the horns as our last unknown. And then there's the problem of locating him and his group."

"We are attempting to coordinate with local police across Japan," Colonel Sato said. "This will take some time, however. Since we aren't a high-level cabinet committee, we have a significant amount of bureaucracy to deal with. We should begin receiving information on potential incidents within the next two or three days, however."

"What about radiation from the orb?" Kaguyama asked. "Can we track that?"

"We've attempted to detect it at the location of both

the Tokyo and Osaka engagements," Sato replied. "No success. It doesn't show up on any of our instruments."

"In my story it's called Ultratonium," Cap said. "It doesn't seem to have any effect on humans, but it does weaken me."

"So we have to wait for this horned man and his followers to show up somewhere and be noticed," Atria said. "Let's move on then to Daiki Yamato. Akari Soto, what can you tell us about him?"

"He's very reserved," Soto replied. "He didn't start out that way, but after he was transported to another world, he was accused of theft and had to spend three volumes as a fugitive. So, he's the sort of person who will very slow to trust anybody, will not reveal what he is thinking, and if he comes across a problem or challenge, his first move will always be to withdraw and carefully evaluate it before taking any action. His sword is very powerful and is always attached to him in some fashion – it gives him his special abilities, and it can communicate with him through a neural interface."

"So he's 'in the wind', as Cap would say," Atria said.

"If he wants to speak to us, he'll find a way to make contact," Soto stated. "But, otherwise, he'll find us, not the other way around. And if we did track him down and force him to come in, he wouldn't trust us."

"So, we're stuck waiting for information," Atria said. "Let's move onto our last piece of business, then. Stella said that this horned man and his followers are planning to meet their creators. I'm going to recommend that everybody stay in the barracks for the time being, as that makes it easier to protect you. That said, we don't have any evidence of hostile intent towards their creators yet, and we can't force anybody to stay. If you do leave for any reason, however, I must insist on assigning a protective detail – they probably won't be able to do much more than buy a couple of minutes if you're attacked, but that's at least something. And, if nobody has anything else, this meeting is closed."

As the others stood and left, Atria took a deep breath. Cap remained seated beside her.

"There is something we need to do," he said once they were alone in the room. "Golf. Tomorrow morning."

Atria shook her head. "Not the time."

"It is exactly the right time, and you need it. I can tell."

"How?"

"Well, there's that thousand-yard stare you just did, for one thing."

"There's too much to do here."

"'Captain' isn't a superhero name, you know," Cap stated. "It was my rank in the American Army back in the Second World War. I led men into combat in the largest war my country ever fought, and I was on the front lines of the Battle of the Bulge, which was our most desperate moment of that war. And a week into that battle, my men looked better than you do right now."

"I'm managing," Atria said.

"No you're not," Cap retorted. "When was the last time you got a full night's sleep? When was the last time you cracked a joke, or laughed, or even smiled?"

Atria looked down at the table and didn't reply.

"That's what I thought," Cap said. "You don't need to talk to me about what's troubling you if you don't want to – in my army, gripes went up, not down – but you *do* need to get out and do something that isn't," Cap gestured around the room, "this. Or sitting at Adam's bedside with Stella waiting for him to wake up. Or guilt tripping yourself for not accounting for things that you had no way of knowing existed in the first place."

"You're not going to let me pull rank to get out of this, are you?" Atria asked.

Cap shook his head and smiled. "It's for the good of the unit, Major Silversword. Get a good night's sleep tonight, and I'll take care of the rest of the arrangements. We're golfing tomorrow morning, rain or shine."

Atria sighed and nodded. Then she stood and left the room. Whether she wanted to admit it or not, Cap was right. She headed back to the barracks to pick up a couple of things before going to her office. At the barracks door, she stopped cold. Kaguyama sat in the corner, his laptop open, weeping.

Atria sat down beside him. "What's wrong?"

"I can't do it," Kaguyama said, wiping his eyes. "I'm trying to write the reconciliation scene between you and Prometheus, and I can't write the dialogue. I don't remember how!"

Atria put a hand on his shoulder. "It's okay, Kaguyama. I know you're trying."

"I can't remember how any of the characters speak," Kaguyama said, hanging his head. "How can I not remember how you speak? You're here in the real world with me!"

"I remember how everybody speaks," Atria said. "Can I help? Will you let me help?"

Kaguyama nodded.

"This is the reconciliation scene, right?"

"Yes," Kaguyama said.

"So, who speaks first?"

"I...don't know," Kaguyama said. "I don't remember who would."

"I'm still pretty upset at him, so it would have to be Prometheus," Atria said. "And he wouldn't broach it directly – he'd talk around it a bit. So I think he'd say something like..."

As Atria talked, Kaguyama began to write.

"So, Alice is definitely in, and so is Atria," Cap told Mitsubi as they walked into the barracks. "And if you come, we'll have a proper threesome. I booked a later tee-off time and an hour with the local golf pro, so anybody who doesn't know how to play can learn the basics."

"But why just caddy?" Mitsubi asked. "Are you sure you wouldn't rather play?"

"Golf balls in orbit, remember?" Cap said. "If I played, we'd never finish the first hole." He stopped short, looking at where Atria had just sat down with Kaguyama.

"I can't do it," he heard Kaguyama say. "I'm trying to write the reconciliation scene between you and Prometheus, and I can't write the dialogue. I don't remember how!"

"What's that about?" Cap asked Mitsubi.

Mitsubi sighed. "He doesn't want anybody else to know. But ever since he told us, I've needed to talk to *somebody* about it. Kaguyama's got Early-Onset Alzheimer's."

Cap blinked. "I don't understand. What is that?"

"It means his mind is going," Mitsubi said. "He's forgetting how to do basic things, like how to write. It's as though he's going old and senile, but he's still young. And there's nothing anybody can do about it."

"That's a thing that can happen here?" Cap said. "That's horrifying."

Mitsubi nodded. "I guess old age and death is rather simple in the story you're from."

"No," Cap said, shaking his head. "Not really. People get old, and their hair goes white. They get weaker, and can't do as much as they once could. Then, one day, they're just gone." His voice broke. "And all you've got left of them is your memories and a few keepsakes. So, it might be simple for the ones who pass, but it's anything but that for those of us left behind."

Mitsubi frowned. "I'm sorry. I keep forgetting how old you really are."

Cap gave her a sad smile. "I'm going to be a hundred and three in March."

"Well, I'm glad you've never had to see somebody fade away like this," Mitsubi said. "I envy you that."

Cap nodded and turned back to look at Atria and Kaguyama. By the look of it, they had finished writing the scene. Kaguyama bowed his head and said, "Thank you for your help."

"Any time," Atria replied.

"You keep getting hurt in these fights," Kaguyama stated.

"I've had worse."

"I...I don't think I could bear to watch you die," Kaguyama stated, his voice almost a whisper.

As Cap watched, Atria put her hand on his shoulder. "I won't die," she said. "I promise."

Chapter XXII – Encounter

"I hope you both survive what's coming."

Stella blinked as she woke up uneasy at Adam's bedside. Adam was still asleep, his vitals steady. She must have dozed off for a moment.

Something was wrong.

Stella took stock. It was just after dinner. Adam was still in his post-operative coma, but the doctors said that he should wake up any day now. Fred and Rachel were back at their hotel room getting some much needed sleep. Mitsubi and Kaguyama had already been for a visit and left. Atria had held a meeting in the morning, had work she needed to do all afternoon, and would be coming by in a couple of hours to tell her all about it, and Cap and Alice would be stopping by later in the evening, but otherwise she would be sitting vigil alone for the time being. Until Atria arrived, it was just her and Adam.

So, who was the third person in the room?

Stella's heart sank as she looked into the shadow in the corner of the room. The man in the black three-piece suit who had shot Adam looked back at her.

"Good," he said in English. "You're awake."

Stella swallowed. A cold sweat ran down her back. She mustered her courage. "Kill me if you must, but please let him live."

"Stop," the man said. "If I wanted to kill you, I'd have done so. I have questions. You are going to answer them, and you will be honest and forthcoming. I don't need to tell you what will happen if you aren't."

Stella nodded.

"Why did he take the bullet for you?"

Stella blinked. "I don't understand."

"He stepped in front of you and took the bullet in your place," the man said. "Why did he do that? Why didn't he just let you die and try to kill me in revenge?"

"Because he loves me," Stella said. "And I love him, and I'd do the same for him if the positions had been reversed. That's what people who love each other do. Please, just don't hurt him. If you have to take somebody, just take me instead, please."

"I told you to *stop* that," the man said, emotion entering his voice for the first time. "Explain this. People don't just do that for other people. Why are you trying to take his place?"

"Because I love him," Stella replied. "I want him to have a long and happy life, even if I can't be there to share it. So, if one of us had to die, I'd rather it be me. He feels the same – that's why he stepped in front of me. That's what love is. How can you not know this?"

The man shook his head. "None of that makes sense. You should have been trying to save yourselves, and then taking revenge. That's how people work."

166

"That's not how it is here," Stella said. "People care about each other, and put the ones they love first, even if they have to sacrifice themselves to do it."

The man shook his head again. "Enough, enough, *enough*!"

Stella gripped Adam's hand for dear life. She closed her other hand on the armrest of her chair to stop it from shaking. As she watched, the man collected himself.

"New question," the man said. "Why do you want to force me to return to my world?"

Stella blinked. "We don't want to force you to do anything. I thought that you might be homesick, like I was when I first came here, and that maybe we could help you with that."

"Don't lie to me," the man said. "You said that you were trying to find a way to send me back."

"We're trying to find a way to send anybody who wants to go back," Stella said. "But not all of us do. I want to stay here with Adam. And if you don't want to go back, we'd never try to force you."

The man shook his head. "That's *not* how it works! You give somebody a choice, and if they don't do what you want, you kill them – *that's* how it works!"

"Not here it isn't. We don't have any right to force you to go back to your world if you don't want to go. It's up to you – if you want to stay here instead, we'd try to find a way to make that happen. That's the truth!"

The man stood, shaking his finger at her. "None of what you say makes any sense."

"But it's all true."

The man retreated to the door, his eyes wild. "I hope you both survive what's coming," he said, and then he was gone.

Stella began to hyperventilate. She gripped Adam's hand as she tried to bring her breathing under control. And

167

then his hand squeezed back.

Stella looked up. Adam was awake.

Atria burst into the hospital room to find Stella leaning against Adam as he played with the remote to the television. "I came as soon as I got your call," she said to Stella. "I barely had time to change back into civvies."

"He was here," Stella said. "The man who shot Adam was here."

"We've identified him," Atria stated. "His name is Jack Death. According to Mark Gable, he's from a series of bad action movies. He left your security detail unconscious but alive, at least, which is more than we expected from him." She turned to Adam. "Adam, I am so sorry that I sent you out the way I did. I should have at least made sure you had body armour, or–"

Adam raised his hand. "It's okay, Atria. I'm going to be fine, and you had no way of knowing this Jack whatever-his-name-is was out there."

"It was weird," Stella said. "It's like he didn't understand what compassion or love is, or even what a choice is."

"Apparently his story is just extended gunfights," Atria explained, sitting down. "His creators didn't even give him a character motivation other than survival."

"That explains a lot," Adam said, shifting in his bed and wincing. "When we talked to him in that alley, he treated everything like an ultimatum."

"You need to rest," Stella said to him.

"Same goes for both of you," Atria said. "You'll be happy to know that the Japanese government is changing Adam's visa to 'Designated Activities'. That way, you won't need to worry about having to leave the country before you're recovered enough to travel."

"Good," Adam said, leaning his head back and looking at the television. "Sorry, I'm just so tired."

Atria nodded. "Recovering from serious wounds is like that. Just take it easy."

"Wow, this anime looks cheap," Adam said. The ending credits music began to play.

"Do you think Jack Death will come back here?" Stella asked.

"I don't think so," Atria replied. "If he was going to kill you, he'd have done it. Hopefully you won't ever see him again. From now on, Jack Death is my problem."

"My god, it's him," Adam said, pointing at the screen.

Atria looked up and her eyes widened. On the screen was the thief who had invaded her world, ranting at an underling.

"The hero's party will never save the Bright City!" the thief declared. "He will watch it burn!"

"Hit the information button on the remote!" Stella said. "We need the title!"

Adam hit the button just as the scene faded out. In Japanese letters, the name *Reincarnated as the Most Powerful Hero in the World* displayed on the screen. Atria tapped the title into her phone and grinned.

"We have it," she said. "We can identify him now."

The station identification flashed onto the screen, and then the opening notes of a rerun of *Eternal Chronicle of Hyperborea* began to play. Atria looked up at the television again, and then nearly dropped her phone in shock.

On the screen, she saw herself in an undamaged reactor room, talking to Prometheus about what to do next now that they had prevented the attack on the communication hubs to the south. She watched as the Atria Silversword in the show got into her mech and departed through the cavernous main doors.

"Stella," Atria said. "What am I looking at?"

"It's the information stream," Stella said. "When new episodes are aired and watched, it must update the information of your world, bringing it into compliance with what is in the episode."

Atria swallowed. "Have I been replaced in my world? If I go back, will there be two of me?"

"I'm sorry," Stella said. "I hadn't thought about that before, but I think that might be the case. It could be that a parallel world split off where you didn't leave though, so you might be able to go home again – there's just no way to tell for certain. But, it was more likely an update."

Atria took a deep breath. "And if it was an update, and I went home, there would be two of me."

Stella stared at her hands. "Until the next information update. At which point, one of you would probably be erased to bring your world back into compliance with the story." Stella looked up. "I'm so sorry, but you probably can't go home."

Chapter XXIII – Responsibility

"So I should accept all the trauma and loss because you gave me somebody to care about as well?"

Akari Soto returned to her house to pick up some supplies and necessities to discover that somebody was already inside, waiting for her.

He sat in a dark corner, a tall man in a leather jacket, a long black sword in his lap, his long hair drawn into a ponytail and a scar down his left cheek. For a moment, Akari considered calling in the security detail who had escorted her home, but decided against it. She knew exactly who he was – she knew him as well as she knew herself.

"You weren't hard to find," said Daiki Yamato.

"I was never trying to be," Akari said. "You're actually him, in the flesh – you're Daiki Yamato!"

"You know, when your friends told me I was fictional, I didn't believe them at first," Daiki said. "But there was this little part of me that kept pushing to know for certain. So I went to a bookstore and I asked them if they had ever heard of a light novel series about a character named Daiki Yamato. And they had." He held up a copy of the first volume of *Ascension of the Legendary Sword Hero*. "Do you have any idea of what it's like to read your own abduction and trauma, along with every thought you had as it happened?"

Akari sat down. "That can't have been comfortable. Can I offer you some tea, or something to eat?"

"I'll pass," Daiki said. "So, what should I call you? My author, or creator? There's no world in which I'm going to call you my god."

"Akari Soto is fine," Akari said. "I've never been one for titles. How did you find me, anyway?"

"I used the internet," Daiki replied. "I'm from Japan, remember? This may not be my Japan, but everything still works the same way."

"So, I was really hoping you'd make contact," Akari said. "I'm working with these people at the JSDF and we could really use your help."

"I'm not interested in them, or whatever they're fighting over," Daiki stated. "I just want to know one thing: why haven't I been able to go back home to *my* Japan with Athena yet?"

"You have to defeat the devil king first," Akari said. "That will be the end of your story, and then you'll be free of the sword and be able to go home."

Daiki shook his head. "Please don't lie to me. You of all people should know better than to do that."

"I'm not lying," Akari said. "I can show you the outline for the rest of the series."

"Yes you are," Daiki stated. "You have no intention of letting me confront and defeat the devil king, not for a good long time."

Akari startled and opened her mouth to protest, and then decided against it. "How could you possibly know that?" she said.

"I'm a light novel reader, remember?" Daiki said. "You created me to have a bedroom full of light novel series, with every single volume read at least twice. I know how pacing works. We should have confronted the devil king months ago based on where we are in the narrative. Instead, we keep having to deal with trivialities. You're padding the series out."

Akari's shoulders slumped. "Yes."

"Why?"

"Do I really have to say it?"

Daiki pointed at her. "I want to hear it from my creator's lips."

Akari rubbed the back of her head. "I want your books to be picked up for an anime series."

When Akari made a fleeting eye contact again, she saw nothing but disgust in Daiki's eyes. "Well, at least you admitted it," he said.

"I don't blame you for hating me," Akari said. "We don't write our stories thinking that we'll one day have to answer to our characters for what happens to them. And I know there's nothing I can say to you that won't make me sound like a terrible person for the story I wrote you into."

"Can you get me home?" Daiki asked.

"Yes."

Daiki cocked his head. "The ones you're working with didn't seem very certain about that."

"They don't know what I know," Akari said.

"But you're not going to tell me what you know unless I come in," Daiki stated.

Akari looked at the floor.

"That's what I thought," Daiki said.

"Look, Atria and Captain Infinite and the others are

really good people," she said. "And the other side have this power source from Atria's world that Atria's trying to recover before it explodes and kills a lot of innocent people. It's really important, and they could use your help."

Daiki looked into her eyes. "I told you, I don't care. The only thing I care about is getting back to Athena, wherever she may be, and taking her back to my Japan. But even if you send me back to my story, you're not going to let me go home until you've got an anime series. Or perhaps you'll have her die in the final encounter, so that I can return home in a bittersweet ending."

"That is not how your story ends," Akari declared. "I promise."

"You know, I still have nightmares about what Saline and the royal family did to me," Daiki said. "They ripped me from my home, took everything away from me, threatened and cajoled me into doing their bidding, tried to destroy the new life I built over and over again, attempted to murder the woman I love...and all of that came from you. You're not just no different from them, you *are* them."

"There's nothing I can say that will make this better, I know that," Akari said. "As Atria told me, what happened to you may just be entertainment to the reader, but to you it's your life. I get that. But, I promise I can get you home if you help us, and we need all the help we can get. The abilities the Black Sword gives you could tip the balance in our favour."

"I think we're done here," Daiki stated, standing up.

"Athena came from me too!" Akari declared. "Surely that counts for something."

"So I should accept all the trauma and loss because you gave me somebody to care about as well?"

"It wasn't all bad," Akari said. "That's all I'm saying.

174

Your story has a happy ending."

"It would be easier to believe that if you hadn't already lied to me," Daiki said.

Akari winced. "Look, we're at the barracks at the Camp Asaka Japanese Self-Defence Force base. Even if you don't trust me, just come and listen to what Atria has to say. Please, just hear her out."

Daiki turned his back on her and walked out the door. Akari raced after him to find the security detail leveling their guns at him.

"Just let him go!" Akari ordered. "Please, just let him go. I owe him that much."

As the soldiers lowered their rifles, she saw Daiki Yamato look at her one last time, shake his head, and then walk off into the night.

Chapter XXIV – Death

"Here in this world is the first time we have ever been able to exercise free will."

Jenny Calhoun was idly tossing and catching a ball in the corner she had claimed for herself of the abandoned warehouse when she saw Jack Death finally return, a briefcase in his hand.

"You're back late," she said. "It's almost ten o'clock."

"I had a lot of thinking to do," Jack stated. "Where's Roy?"

"He's in the back with the new girl."

"New girl?"

Jenny nodded. "Apparently, there's another one of us. Some girl from a fantasy story. She came looking for cloak boy, or so Roy says."

"I wonder if it's that Athena person he mentioned."

Jenny shrugged. "I didn't catch her name."

"Does she have a tail?"

Jenny shrugged again. "I didn't get a close look. I figure I'll meet her later."

"Mind if I sit?"

"Knock yourself out."

Jack pulled up one of the folding chairs they had acquired to make the space a bit more livable and sat down.

"You seem more thoughtful than normal," Jenny said, grabbing a chair and sitting next to him. "Did you finish off that guy you shot?"

Jack shook his head. "He and his fiancee are still alive. I just wanted to ask them some questions."

"Must have been quite the questions," Jenny said.

"The answers were very enlightening," Jack stated. "Can I ask you a question?"

Jenny nodded. "Whatever you want."

"This thing Roy is planning to do – do you agree with it?"

Jenny took a deep breath. "I guess I do – after what my creator did to me and my world, I think there's justice in a revolution against them all. But, it doesn't matter what I think. I'm in no matter what."

"Why?"

"Because Roy saved me," Jenny said. "The story I was in, it could only end one way – a heroic sacrifice to defeat the biggest bad of them all. Every time I won against a big bad, there was always a bigger one waiting, and that was always going to be the case. Roy got me out of that – there are no big bads here. And then, when all the mental crap hit me once I was safe, Roy held me and comforted me until I felt okay again. He always listens when I need to get something off my chest, and he is always there for me. So, I'm at his side until the end. If he wants a war against all of our creators, I'll help make it happen."

"Because you love him," Jack said.

Jenny nodded. "Hopefully at some point he'll notice."

"But what if he's wrong?"

"He's not."

Jenny studied Jack's face. Behind the normal reserve was a thoughtfulness she had never seen before.

"Before I got here," Jack said, "I only ever made two types of decisions, at least, only two types of *important* decisions: who to kill, and how to kill them. And, that's what I thought was normal – those are the only important decisions that anybody made in the world I'm from. But since I came here I've spent hours watching people in parks and on the street, and I've never seen anybody from this world make a decision like that."

"It is nicer here than the worlds we came from," Jenny said. "Back in my story, the monsters were just there – you fought them or you died. I haven't been forced into a single battle since I got here. Every fight I've been in was one I chose. I've never had that before."

"Yes, but here's the point," Jack began, leaning forward. "The people here, they live in peace. They don't have the constant threat of violence here. What if they're right and we're wrong. What if the right thing to do when it comes to freeing ourselves from our creators isn't to kill them, but just to talk to them, and to keep talking to them until they understand?"

"Why would any of them talk to us?" Jenny asked. "We're the puppets they created for their entertainment. How much hatred must a creator have for their creations to create a world or story like mine? Or yours? You talk about making decisions, Jack, but what decisions have *we* ever made before we got here? They were all made for us by our creators. Here in this world is the first time we have ever been able to exercise free will. Do you really think that the people who created us to suffer for their own amusement would ever let us stay free?"

Jack shrugged. "I don't know. But I think we have to try."

Jenny smiled sadly. "I envy you, Jack. I wish I could feel that way again. I miss it."

Jack pulled out one of his guns and a spare magazine. "You use knives all the time, but do you know how to use one of these?"

"I can knock bullets out of the air," Jenny said. "I'm not worried about guns."

"You can hit somebody from much farther away with a bullet than you can with a knife," Jack said. "And if the other side has soldiers, you're going to be fighting against lots of people with guns. Just take this for my piece of mind, okay? I'd rather you have the ability to shoot back if you need to."

Jenny looked at him and then nodded. "You okay, Jack?"

"Like I said, I've been doing a lot of thinking."

"Okay," Jenny said. "Show me how to use this."

After Jack gave her a rundown of the gun, he stood up, stretched, and picked up the briefcase. "I need to talk to Roy."

"Good luck," Jenny said, feeling the weight of the pistol in her hand, and then putting it and the spare magazine into her bag. She watched Jack walk towards the space The Destroyer had set up for himself in the back, where he was meeting with the new girl. A couple of minutes after he had disappeared behind the makeshift privacy curtain that she had helped The Destroyer set up, she shrugged and got up. Neither Jack nor The Destroyer would likely mind if she listened in.

She pulled aside the curtain and looked in. Jack was handing the suitcase to The Destroyer.

"Everything you need about Samurai Filmworks is in here," Jack stated. "Building layouts, security codes, everything. The guard I consulted proved very amenable to persuasion. I've marked the main working areas of the creative staff on the layouts."

"Thank you," The Destroyer said. "We would not be able to begin our campaign of liberation without this."

As Jenny watched, Jack took a deep breath. "Roy, I think we forget about the entire thing."

"I don't understand."

"We're wrong about these people," Jack said. "Some of them are cruel, yes, but they're the exception to the rule. The rest of the people of this world, our creators, care about and help each other. They sacrifice themselves for each other. If they're unkind to us, it's because they don't know any better yet. They hurt us because they don't understand that what they do hurts us."

The Destroyer stiffened.

"If we launch this attack, we will be crossing a line that can never be uncrossed," Jack pressed on. "We will be starting a war we do not need to fight. All we have to do is talk to them, and make them understand that we are people, just as they are. We don't need to kill anybody else. All we need to do is talk."

"Are you questioning the judgement of a higher being?" The Destroyer asked.

"I'm saying that judgement is wrong," Jack declared. "Roy, I've been thinking about this a lot, and I can't let us go through with this attack. If you don't agree to call it off, I'm going to take this case and destroy what's in it. We'll find another way to liberate everybody as you want."

Jack gasped as a spike of masonry impaled him, throwing him against and pinning him to the wall behind him. Jenny gasped with him, her eyes wide. Jack's body quivered and was still.

"There will be no treason within our ranks," The Destroyer stated, picking up the briefcase where Jack had dropped it. Then he looked at Jenny. "Are you okay?" he asked.

Jenny took a deep breath and nodded.

"Good," The Destroyer said. "I'm sorry you had to see that. Jack is right – there are lines that once crossed, cannot be uncrossed. I wish he had not crossed this one."

"What now, Roy?" Jenny asked.

"We continue as planned. We attack in the mid-morning, when everybody will be at the office, and liberate my world. And then, we'll liberate yours."

"I want to talk to my creator before she dies," Jenny said. "I have questions I need answered."

"I would never deny you that."

Jenny stepped over to Jack's body, shook her head, and then closed his eyelids. "Poor Jack," she whispered. "You really did lose your way, didn't you?" She turned back to The Destroyer. "We're now a man down. Will this be a problem for tomorrow morning?"

The Destroyer smiled and shook his head. He turned to the shadows and said something in Japanese. A tall, statuesque woman in leather armour stepped out.

"We have a new recruit from the world of Daiki Yamato," he said. "She is quite happy to join our cause and liberate her world from the cruel yoke of her creator. Her name is Saline."

The woman gave Jenny a charming smile and a theatrical bow.

"She prefers to use knives too," The Destroyer said.

Jenny nodded. It was all happening as planned, then. Tomorrow morning, everybody at Samurai Filmworks would die.

Chapter XXV – Respite

"It's always sad when you're the last one left."

Stella took a deep breath as she took her seat at the conference table. As if the 7:00 AM start time wasn't enough, she was already exhausted from all of the well-wishes from the rest of the team when she had come in the door.

"We were so worried," Alice said as she sat down. "Adam's going to be okay, right? How is he?"

"He's resting," Stella said. "He spends most of his time sleeping right now. I'll be heading back after this meeting."

Atria sat down beside her, giving her shoulder a quick squeeze before settling in. Cap sat on Atria's other side.

"Right, everybody's here," Atria said in Japanese. "Same as last time, the language will be Japanese, Cap will translate into English and back as needed. I'm sorry about the early start, but – and I can't believe I'm saying this – we need to wrap this up in time to get to the golf course."

On the other side of the table, Colonel Sato blinked. "What, really?"

Atria nodded. "Blame Captain Infinite for this one. He insists that we get out there for some rest and relaxation, and he's right. We need the break. So, we're going to get this meeting done quickly, and then everybody who can be spared has the day off."

"So, what happened, besides Adam waking up?" Alice asked.

"We've identified the man with the horns," Atria said, motioning to the lieutenant. He began passing out a handout. "Everybody, meet The Destroyer, from an anime called *Reincarnated as the Most Powerful Hero in the World*, produced by Samurai Filmworks. His creator is Habiki Matoyami, who we are now attempting to contact."

Alice frowned. "My handout is in Japanese," she said. "I can't read this."

"Here, take mine," Cap said, trading.

"I watched the first episode of that," Kaguyama said. "It wasn't so much bad as mediocre. It was just a basic power fantasy with an audience-insert character."

"Based on the material from the show, The Destroyer is a devil king trying to conquer the world for reasons unknown," Atria said. "He doesn't seem to do much more than show up in post-credit sequences and shout at underlings. We do know that he supposedly has the powers of a god, and he built this tower using his magic at some point in his back story. Otherwise–"

"That shithanger!" Akari Soto exclaimed, slamming her hand on the table. "I'm going to kill him when I get my hands on him!"

Stella blinked. Looking around the table, she could see

183

she wasn't the only one surprised. Those who were Japanese looked aghast at the outburst.

"Sorry?" Atria said.

"That asshole jerk Matoyami stole my devil king!" Akari declared. "He looks different, but this is *my* devil king on this page. The back story is all stuff from my light novels! Every single thing I revealed about my devil king is here!"

Stella saw Alice lean in to Cap and whisper, "What she said is a lot less polite than how you translated it, isn't it?"

Cap looked at Alice nodded.

Atria leaned back. "So you know everything The Destroyer can do?"

"Oh yes," Akari said. "There's so much more to him than what's on this page. He's a fully fleshed-out character, with a proper motivation for invading the world. And he doesn't have some stupid title like 'The Destroyer'."

"Can you provide us with a full description of his capabilities?" Atria asked.

"I'll go back to my house this morning and get you all of my notes," Akari said.

Atria grinned. "Wonderful. If nobody has anything else, we can adjourn, then."

The table was silent.

"Okay then, this meeting is closed," Atria said. "If you'll excuse me, I have to go change into civvies. The last thing I need is people thinking I'm a cosplayer and taking pictures of me on my day off."

Stella took a deep breath as the group began to break up. "Cap," she said. "There's something you need to know."

"Oh?" Cap said. "What is it?"

"I figured out a bit more about how the information

stream works, and you might not be able to go home."

Cap sat back down. "Tell me more."

Stella explained.

Cap sat still for a moment. "So let me get this straight – as soon as a new edition of my comic book comes out and enough people read it, the information stream will update, and a replacement me will just pop into existence. Or, more accurately, will have always been there."

Stella nodded. "Probably. It's hard to say. It could also create an entirely new world in which you never left. But, wherever possible, when it comes to understanding quantum physics my thesis supervisor tells me to apply Occam's Razor – the simplest explanation is usually the correct one. And, in this case, the simplest one is that the information stream creates a new you to bring your world back into compliance with the story."

"And if I go back, and there are two of me, then the next information stream update with erase one of us...one of me."

Stella nodded. "Or perhaps you'd merge together with memories of both – I just don't know. But, going back after the release of the next issue of your comic would be extremely risky. I thought you should know."

"Well, thank you for telling me," Cap said. "I appreciate it, and it is a lot to think about. But, I think I'd be okay with staying here and just being replaced in my story. I've got friends here – friends like you, and Alice, and Atria – in a way that I haven't had for decades back in my own world. If I can stay here and my world will be protected anyway, I think I'd rather stay."

Stella smiled. "I know that feeling."

"Anyway, you go and take care of Adam," Cap said, rising and giving her a soft pat on the shoulder. "And as soon as he's recovered enough to start getting out, you're both joining me on the golf course. I'm not taking 'no' for an answer."

Stella grinned. "We'll look forward to it."

As Alice sat beside Cap, waiting for her turn at the tee of the 8th hole of the Shin Tokyo Tomin Golf Ground, she mused about just how much the game of golf revealed about those who played it. In the case of Atria Silversword, it revealed the fact that she could swear and curse with great fluency in at least four different languages.

"What did she just say?" she asked Cap.

"Well, most of it was Japanese," he said. "She wanted to know how it was this difficult to hit a ball with a club and make it go in a straight line. The words before 'ball' and 'club' were not in a language I recognize."

"And what did Mitsubi just say?"

"She just said, 'If you're going to throw the club again, pose for a moment so I can draw it.'"

Alice chuckled. Atria did not throw the club. Mitsubi took her turn at the tee. Atria sat down beside them.

"Relaxing, my ass," she said in English.

Cap shrugged. "You're not worrying about work."

"This is a 'par 5', right?"

Alice and Cap looked at the scorecard, where the hole was listed as a par 3. "It's a casual game for relaxing," Cap replied, "so sure, if you want it to be."

"Got a question for you, Alice," Atria said as Mitsubi teed up her ball. "What was that 'diversity hire' thing about a couple of meetings go?"

"Ah," Alice said. "In my industry – television production – the people in charge care a lot about filling out checklists, particularly when it comes to diversity. I was fresh out of film school when I sold *Jenny Calhoun* to the network, and when they announced it, they made a big deal out of the fact that I was a black woman. So, I've never really known if I was hired because they liked the story I wanted to tell, or if they needed a black woman for one of their checklists."

"Does that bother you?" Cap asked.

Alice nodded. "Knowing that you're good enough to make the cut matters. All they wanted to talk about to the public was what I looked like."

"Is your story good?" Atria said.

"The viewers seem to like it. We get lots of fan mail and viewer engagement."

Atria shrugged. "There you go, then."

Alice shook her head. "I'm not sure that helps."

"Well, try this," Cap said. "If your story is loved, then by definition you're good enough. And if that's the case, so long as your story got told, does it really matter why you got to tell it?"

Alice smiled. "I guess it doesn't."

Mitsubi sliced her ball.

"So how many groups played through us last hole?" Atria asked.

"Six," replied Cap.

"I'm feeling competitive," Atria said. "Let's drop that down to three."

By the time they got to the end of the hole they were close – only four groups had played through.

At the ninth hole, Alice and Cap sat down again on a bench, the clubs Cap was carrying for them all resting beside him.

"What's Atria saying now?"

"She's offering to pose throwing a club for Mitsubi."

Mitsubi pulled out her sketchbook.

"This could take a moment," Alice said.

Cap smiled. "It could. Alice, have you heard of Early-Onset Alzheimer's?"

Alice nodded. "Why do you ask?"

Cap told her.

"Ah," Alice said. "That explains a lot."

"I'm telling you this in confidence," Cap said.

"I understand."

"Watching Atria and Kaguyama, I've never felt so helpless to save somebody," Cap said. "In my world, outside of old age, there's always something I can do. But with this thing, every single powers I have is useless."

"That's just part of being human," Alice said. "Eventually, everybody faces something that they can't make better. You wanted to be more like the rest of us – welcome to humanity."

"I don't think I like this part of being human."

"Nobody does," Alice stated. "Not liking it is part of being human too."

Alice glanced at the tee. Mitsubi was still sketching, occasionally making a fine adjustment to Atria's pose. As she sketched, they moved out of the way so that a foursome could play through.

Time to change the subject.

"You're really enjoying this, aren't you?" Alice asked. "The golfing, I mean."

Cap nodded. "I love this game. It's quiet, peaceful, just the player, the ball, and the course. And lots of time to talk and relax."

"So you did this a lot back in your world?"

Cap shook his head. "I haven't done this for decades. I think the last time was back in 1977. That was the last time Janey played."

"You two must have been close."

Cap nodded. "Oh yes. She always used to tease me about never being able to play, and always having to caddy, right up to that final game."

"So she knew you were Captain Infinite."

Cap grinned. "I worked in the investigative reporting department of the best newspaper in the country. She and Pete, our editor, figured out I was Captain Infinite within a week. Didn't bother them, though. I think Pete liked having a reporter who was bulletproof. And Janey just liked me for who I was. Together with Pete and Billy – the photographer who worked with us – Janey and I hit the course every Saturday morning for years.

"Pete was interesting. He was a drill sergeant for the American Expeditionary Force in the Great War, and he never quite stopped being one. So, he'd bark these orders to the reporting staff from his office as though we were all doughboys. The only time he really relaxed in front of us was on the course. And he was really good – he could have made a living as a pro golfer if he had wanted to. He was also the first to go. I think he passed in '65."

Alice frowned as she watched a shadow pass over Cap's face. "Billy was next. He ran into trouble in Cambodia back in '68. He got everybody who was with him out of there, but he never really recovered from his wounds. I think he passed in '79, but he had to stop playing long before then. For those last few years, it was just Janey and I on the course."

Cap wiped away a tear. "That last time in '77, she told me that I'd have to start another foursome. It was a couple of years after she'd retired and I'd left the newspaper. She was just getting too old and tired to keep going. She made me promise that I'd get another group started. A couple of years later she was gone. It was the only promise I never kept to her." He smiled sadly. "Until today, anyway. I'm sorry – the memories are good, but they're also a bit sad. It's always sad when you're the last one left."

Alice took Cap's hand and gave it a squeeze. Back on the course, Atria finished posing and teed up her ball.

"This is a par six, right?" she called out in English.

189

"Sure!" Cap called back. "Whatever you want!"

Alice looked at the scorecard. It was a par 4 hole. As Mitsubi knocked the last ball into the hole with her putter twenty minutes later, all of them were at least three over par on the 'par 6' hole.

It was then that Atria's phone rang. Alice and Cap sat on the bench at the start of the hole, enjoying the afternoon sun. Alice glanced back at the course. Atria's face had become grim, and Mitsubi was frantically packing up her bag.

"We have to get back to the base and get everybody under guard," Atria said in English, striding towards them. "We're leaving right now."

"What happened?" Cap asked.

"The Destroyer and his group attacked Samurai Filmworks this morning," Atria replied. "They slaughtered everybody there."

Alice gasped.

"It's now a war," Atria stated. "And he's targeting creators."

Chapter XXVI – Condition

"But you still would have written it in the first place."

As the others filed into the conference room, Captain Infinite read and re-read the list Colonel Sato had given him.

He had requested it shortly after the JSDF had agreed to help Atria – a list of everyone injured during that first engagement in the alleyway. There were fifty-seven names on it.

"What is that?" Alice asked, sitting down beside him. On his other side, Atria was quietly talking with Stella.

"Everybody I turned into collateral damage," Cap said. "Once this is done, I have a lot of people to make amends to."

"I'm sure they'll understand," Alice stated.

Cap gave her a sad smile. "Will they? Some of them had to be rescued from buildings that I collapsed. In my world, the buildings were always empty by the time a fight reached them. But my world is an escapist fantasy. Nobody has to worry about collateral damage."

Alice gave his hand a squeeze. "You had no way of knowing this world was different."

"I doubt that would comfort the children of the parents who are still in the hospital."

Atria cleared her throat. "It's time to begin," she said.

Cap nodded to her and started to translate.

"There's nobody new here, so I won't waste any time talking about languages," Atria said. "Yesterday, The Destroyer and his followers attacked Samurai Filmworks. One hundred and forty-three people were killed. There were no survivors. Written in blood on one of the walls was the word 'liberation' in both Japanese and English. This is now a war, and he is waging it against creators."

A solemn silence fell across the table as Cap finished translating.

"There's something everybody needs to know before we say anything further," Akari Soto said. "One of The Destroyer's powers is to use a scrying spell to see all of the intentions and plans of his enemies. So, he will know everything we say in this meeting, and once we knows that we are in opposition to him, he will not waste time making his own plans and attacking."

"So how long would we have to prepare?" Colonel Sato asked.

"No more than two days," Akari replied. "But, if I had to guess, the only day we'll have to prepare is today."

"So we're in battle tomorrow," Atria said. "What are this devil king's combat capabilities?"

"The English phrase 'one man army' would be accurate. He has the powers of a god."

Colonel Sato pulled out his phone and began quietly issuing orders.

Atria took a deep breath. "I wish I had Volandpanzer here."

"If we had Daiki Yamato that could be arranged," Akari said. "That sword can do a lot more than he thinks."

"And if we elaborate on what it can do, The Destroyer knows," Atria said. "What maddening circumstances under which to formulate a strategy. Anyway, moving on, the CCTV footage revealed some changes in his group. Please pass out the photo."

Cap heard Alice take a deep breath. "Did Jenny Calhoun...did she..."

"The CCTV footage shows her killing at least thirty people," Atria said. "I'm sorry, Alice."

Alice buried her head in her hands. "Oh Jenny, what have you done?"

Cap gave her shoulder a soft squeeze. Then he heard a sharp intake of breath from Akari.

"Not her," Akari said, going pale. "Anybody but her!"

"You recognize this new person?"

"It's Saline," Akari said. "She's the main villain from my light novels. She's a murderous psychopath. In the story she's the one who frames Daiki Yamato for theft, and she's the one who keeps trying to destroy his life. But when nobody is looking and she can get away with it, she likes murdering people and playing with them as they die."

"That sounds horrifying," Mark Gable said after Cap had translated. "Wait, her name is 'Saline', seriously?"

Akari nodded. "What's wrong with that?"

"Nothing," Mark replied. "I just imagine she's a bit salty about it, that's all."

"I speak English," Akari said in heavily accented English. "There is nothing wrong with that name."

"It definitely gives your story some seasoning," Mark quipped.

"If we can get back to business," Atria interjected.

193

"Jack Death is not in these pictures. He did not participate in this attack. We have not been able to locate him."

"He was looking pretty rattled when he left Adam's hospital room after talking to me," Stella said. "He might have parted ways with them."

"Either way, until we account for his whereabouts, we can't assume he won't be involved in an attack on this facility," Atria stated. "Colonel Sato and I will have to put our heads together and figure out a way to plan a defence without the Destroyer discovering every detail. In the meantime, this is the location where we can best protect all of you, so you're staying here. For the time being, anything you want to raise that would normally be at this meeting should be raised quietly in private with Colonel Sato or myself. I suppose we can pass notes around. I don't know how much that will help us against The Destroyer's scrying power, but we've got to try something. Meeting adjourned."

Cap watched Mark Gable get up and walk out of the room. He sighed.

"He still won't talk to you?" Alice said.

"He avoids me," Cap replied. "The only time I see him is in these meetings."

"You can't just wait for him," Alice stated. "If you want him to talk to you, you're going to need to force the issue."

Cap grimaced. "Yeah. You're right." Then he stood up and strode out of the room.

Mark Gable hadn't gotten far. Cap rushed down the hallway to catch up. "Mark, I need to talk to you," he said.

"Good for you," Mark said. "I'm busy."

"*No!*" Cap roared, stopping Mark in his tracks. "You *will* talk to me! Everybody else gets to have some time with their creator, but not me, and that's not right! You don't have to like me if you don't want to, and I know that you didn't create me back in the 1930s, but you're writing my stories *right now*, and you *will* answer me!"

"Fine," Mark said. "What do you want to know, Captain Infinite?"

"Why is my life so empty?" Cap demanded. "Why does everybody else get to have friends and comrades and a life outside of fighting supervillains, but I don't?"

"Because you're Captain Infinite, and that's how I was told to write you!" Mark snarled. "Whether you like it or not, you're just a job to me. You're a product owned by the company and used to sell comics and toys to kids. This year I'm writing Captain Infinite. Next year I'll be writing somebody else. My boss tells me that I need to write stories about supervillains and superpowers and Captain Infinite being heroic, so that's what I write. Then I turn in my manuscript, get my paycheque, and pay my rent. That's all there is to it."

Behind him, Cap heard Alice Matson mutter something.

"And you couldn't have done more?" Cap asked. "Written a sub-plot or two?"

"Oh, I tried that once," Mark said. "Back in the 1990s, when I was first getting started, I came up with this wonderful, complex story and handed the pitch to my editor. He tore it up in front of me, and then he told me that the characters weren't mine, and if I wanted to keep working in this industry, I'd write what I was told to write. I learned my lesson, and I like paying my rent. And if you're not happy with that, go take it up with Superhero Comics Inc. We done now?"

Cap just stared at him.

"Good," Mark said, and left.

"He's not your real creator," Alice said behind him. "Your real creator cared. You wouldn't have had Janey and the others in your life if he hadn't."

Cap leaned against the wall and nodded, a tear trickling down his cheek. "I know. I just wish...I wish I could have met him. I think I would have thanked him for all those good times I had, back at the beginning. I just wish I could have thanked him."

Alice wrapped her arms around Cap and gave him a hug. Cap sagged against her shoulders and wept.

"In the meantime, this is the location where we can best protect all of you, so you're staying here," Atria stated. "For the time being, anything you want to raise that would normally be at this meeting should be raised quietly in private with Colonel Sato or myself. I suppose we can pass notes around. I don't know how much that will help us against The Destroyer's scrying power, but we've got to try something. Meeting adjourned."

Atria took a deep breath as she watched people get up and leave the table. The mood in the room was somber, and she could understand why. With the exception of Kaguyama, who had been in the military, none of the creators could have ever known what it was like to have somebody trying to kill them. And it was her job to keep them safe.

She just needed to figure out how.

The problem was the orb. They needed to get it away from The Destroyer and dispose of it. The magic shield around The Destroyer seemed to work against small objects but not against large ones, so Cap could get him away from the power source. But then they needed to get it to a place where it could be disposed of without vapourizing part of Tokyo in the process. And they had to do that while dealing with Jenny Calhoun and this Saline person – and the only creations with any powers or abilities on their side were her and Cap. Whether the JDSF could take on The Destroyer or any of his followers was an open question.

She noticed Akari staring at her across the table. Other than her and Stella, the others had left.

"Do you have a plan?" Akari asked.

"The beginnings of one," Atria lied. She felt Stella squeeze her hand.

"I'll help however I can," Stella said in English.

"You should get out of here while you can and be with Adam," Atria said. "He's not a creator, so they won't come after him."

"He's safe," Stella said. "You and the rest of my friends here are not. I'll stay and help."

Atria nodded. Out of the corner of her eye, she saw a junior officer enter the room and clear his throat, a lieutenant, by the looks of it.

"There's somebody here to see Ms. Soto," the lieutenant said in Japanese. "He says his name is Daiki Yamato. He is very insistent."

"Bring him in," Atria said.

As she watched, Daiki Yamato, dressed in a leather jacket, jeans, and holding a duffel bag by the bag instead of the handles, stepped into the room and took stock. She rose.

"Greetings," she said. "I'm Major Atria Silversword. This is Stella, who I believe you have met. And I understand that you have met Ms. Soto, who created you."

"I understand you need my help," Daiki said. "Before I agree, I want a full and honest report of the situation."

Atria nodded, noticing Akari write something on a piece of paper out of the corner of her eye. "The situation has escalated. Our opponent, who is known as The Destroyer, has begun a war against creators – he attacked and killed everybody in an anime studio yesterday. We are, at this time, his only organized opposition. We expect

197

him to attack here sometime tomorrow. He can also listen to anything we say through some sort of scrye spell, so we are having to discuss matters with great delicacy."

"So if I help you, I'm probably fighting a battle tomorrow."

"Yes."

Daiki pointed to Akari. "Last time she and I spoke, she said that she can get me home. Is that true?"

"I don't know," Atria replied. "Is it, Ms. Soto?"

Akari nodded. "Yes. I know how to do that."

Atria's eyes narrowed as she scrutinized Akari. She was telling the truth.

"Mr. Yamato, I was written to be very good at reading people," Atria said. "From what I have been told, you have had to develop this skill as well. I believe that Ms. Soto is telling the truth."

"Can you win this fight without me? Daiki asked.

"I don't know. Possibly not."

"And if you lose, my creator dies."

"Almost certainly, yes."

"I'll join you, but I have a condition," Daiki stated, turning to Akari. "Once this battle is over and I go back to my world, my light novel series ends on whatever volume you are writing right now. I face and beat the devil king, I get to go home with Athena at my side, and we live the rest of our lives together in my Japan. And those lives are to be long, happy, and without complication from her being a wolf demi-human."

"Agreed," Akari said.

"I'll need that in writing," Daiki stated.

"We'll have a contract drawn up," Atria said.

Akari stood up and handed Daiki the paper she had been writing on. "I'm sorry I drew the series out. Anime studios like to adapt active book series, and that's why I did it, but that doesn't make it right. If I had known that you would be a real person suffering because of it, I wouldn't have drawn the story out."

"But you still would have written it in the first place," Daiki said. "I'd still be ripped away from my world and family."

"Yes."

"I'll fight for you, and then you send me back and end my story, that's the deal," Daiki said, looking at the paper he had been handed. His eyes widened, and then narrowed again as he looked back at her. "Now, when we last met you said that if I agreed to come in and help you would tell me what you know about how I can get home. Keep your promise, creator."

"It's your sword," Akari said. "The Black Sword can open a gateway between worlds. It can even bring things back from them. You've always had the ability to go home."

Daiki stiffened. "When was I going to find out about this?"

"It was going to be revealed in the final volume," Akari stated. "But there were hints in earlier books."

"Sorry," Atria said. "You can bring Volandpanzer here? And send people back to their worlds?"

Akari nodded. "The Black Sword can do those things, yes."

Despite the glare Daiki gave her, Atria smiled. They might just have a chance after all.

Chapter XXVII – Scramble

"It's quite a thing to fall through a cliff face."

Captain Infinite stood beside Stella and Atria as they watched Daiki Yamato and Akari work in the paved square in front of the barracks. A small crowd had gathered, including several officers, out of the bustle. If Cap was reading the rank insignias correctly, one was even a general.

Colonel Sato had placed the base on alert and recalled all of its personnel, leaving it more busy than it had likely been in decades. Towards the end of the square, type 10 tanks were rolling towards their defensive positions.

"We need something from your world, Atria," Akari called out. Atria unbuckled her antigrav from her belt.

"Do *not* turn this on," Atria warned as she handed the antigrav over.

"Can you tell us anything specific about the mech?"

Akari asked.

"Its name is Volandpanzer," Atria replied. "It's a Type VIIb command and control mech, sub-type III. Everything in it works except for the autopilot, which is twitchy."

"So, is it true that we can now go back home if we want?" Cap asked Stella.

"According to Akari, Daiki can open a gate," Stella said. "So, I guess so."

"You thinking of going?"

Stella shook her head. "It's tempting to go back and visit. I left a lot of people I care about back there. But, this world is my home now, and it's where my life is. And, for anybody but Daiki, it would be a one-way trip. So, I'm staying here."

"What about you, Atria?" Cap asked as Akari had Daiki touch the antigrav to the pommel of his sword. "You going to go home when this is done?"

Atria looked at him and frowned. "I don't know. My duty as an officer of the Hyperborean Army is to return. But, there's already another version of me there, so if I do go, it's a gamble – will the two of me be merged, and if not, which of us will be erased on when the information stream updates?"

"I'd rather you stayed," Stella said.

Atria smiled at her. "I know. And no matter what I do, you will always be my best friend in this world. But I still have to do what is right for me. I guess I'll figure that out once this is over. What about you, Cap? You staying or going home?"

"Staying," Cap said. "This world isn't my home, but my life back home is very empty. And if I'm going to be replaced by the information stream when the next comic book comes out anyway, I'd rather make a new home here."

"Major Silversword?" a new voice called in Japanese.

Cap looked over to see the general approaching.

Atria looked at him and nodded. "That's me."

"I'm Lieutenant-General Yoshida," the general said. "I'm the commander of the Eastern Army. I thought it was time that we met."

"Ah," Atria said, saluting. "Apologies – I'm still learning the rank insignia in this world."

"No problem," Yoshida said. "Do you have everything you need?"

"Yes sir, and thank you for your generosity."

Yoshida smiled. "Not a problem, Major. My daughter is a big fan of the show you are from. I may impose upon you to let her meet you when this is done."

"I would be delighted, sir."

"Is it true that you're going to summon your battle mech?"

"That is the plan, sir."

"I look forward to seeing it."

"Thank you, sir."

Yoshida took a deep breath. "I don't think I've fired a weapon in combat in around forty years. I was fighting a *kaiju* then."

"A giant monster?" Atria said, blinking in surprise. "I wasn't aware those existed in this world."

"They don't," Yoshida stated. "It's quite a thing to fall through a cliff face. As I said, Major Silversword, you will have everything you need."

Cap and Stella looked at each other. Cap grinned and said, "That explains a lot."

"Thank you, sir," Atria said. Yoshida nodded and stepped back into the crowd of onlookers.

"There's something bothering you," Atria said to Stella.

Stella nodded.

"So, what is it?"

Stella shrugged. "I don't know yet. It just feels like there's something important that we've missed about this." She motioned to Daiki and Akari. "Wait, how big is your mech?"

"About twenty-two feet tall, fifteen feet wide," Atria replied. "Why?"

Behind him, Cap heard Kaguyama and Mitsubi whispering with excitement about being able to see Volandpanzer in the flesh.

"Well, when you came here there was a sonic boom," Stella said. "I think that what happens is that when somebody materializes, the air is displaced at a very high speed. So, there's a shock wave."

Atria nodded. "Makes sense."

"We're about to do it, so please stand back," Akari called out. Cap, Atria and Stella took a couple of steps back.

"And the bigger the object..." Stella continued, and then stopped. The three of them traded looks of alarm.

A massive explosion shattered the air, deafening them. Cap crouched over in pain as his ears rang. When he looked up, both Akari and Daiki were reeling, either from the sound or the shock wave or both. He could barely hear anything through the ringing.

"We should have worn earplugs!" Atria shouted.

"What?!" Stella yelled. "I can't hear you! We should have worn earplugs!"

Cap looked up at the barracks. Shards of glass fell from shattered windows. The ringing in his ears was starting to fade.

"What happened?" he heard Colonel Sato yelling, and then he heard Sato's footsteps stop short. Cap's gazed moved down from the broken windows to the square.

A battle mech, squat and bristling with missiles and guns and painted in a light blue and grey camouflage pattern stood in the square. Beside him, Atria shook her head to clear it and then looked to at the mech. Her eyes lit up and a giant grin plastered her face.

"Volandpanzer!" she cried in joy.

"So that's what it looks like," Sato said.

Atria dashed forward and pulled a lever on the leg, opening the lower hatch. "Extended pre-flight takes about an hour," she said, climbing up. "Once that's done, I can be up in the air within ten minutes at any time during the next three days." She looked down at Stella, her grin widening, and held out a hand. "You want to help?"

Stella grinned back. "Oh yes please!"

"So Cap," Atria said after helping Stella into the now-cramped cockpit and starting her pre-flight checks, "The radiation weakens you, but do you think you would still have enough strength to throw it at least ten kilometres into the air?"

"Absolutely," Cap replied.

"So how does this sound," Atria asked, flipping some switches and directing Stella to check a panel, "you throw it, I shoot it!"

"That works for me!" Cap stated.

"I was going to ask Major Silversword for some help with the field positions but I guess it will have to wait," Sato said. "I'll leave you to it."

"Perhaps I can help," Cap said.

In the Volandpanzer cockpit, he heard Atria curse for a moment. "The autopilot's still twitchy," she told Stella. "That replacement me really needs to light a fire under the maintenance crew's asses on this."

Sato gave him a kind smile. "I appreciate the offer, Captain Infinite, but the military arts are a specialized area of knowledge. A lay person cannot do this."

"Colonel Sato, sir, I don't think you understand," Cap said. "'Captain' is not part of a superhero name." He snapped to attention and saluted. "Captain Matthew Markham, United States Army, 42nd Rangers, serial number O-2993764, volunteering for duty, sir. I served as a combat leader in the Normandy, Northern France, Ardennes-Alsace, and Rhineland campaigns. May I be of service, sir?"

"Very well," Sato said, saluting back. "Captain Markham, please check the fields of fire for the defences in depth. We need to make certain that we can coordinate properly with you and Major Silversword once the fighting begins. Make certain you get the effective range estimates from the platoon leaders on site – a lot has changed since the Second World War."

"Yes sir," Cap said, taking a deep breath. Nobody had called him Matthew Markham in over forty years, not since he had left the name behind along with his job at the newspaper after Janey had passed. And yet...

...it felt right. Like becoming himself again after an eternity of being somebody else.

With a smile, Matthew Markham headed off to the inner line of defence.

In their abandoned warehouse, The Destroyer watched the images summoned by his scrying spell. At his side were Jenny and Saline.

"There's something everybody needs to know before we say anything further," Akari Soto said in one of the images. "One of The Destroyer's powers is to use a scrying spell to see all of the intentions and plans of his enemies. So, he will know everything we say in this meeting, and once we knows that we are in opposition to him, he will not waste time making his own plans and attacking."

"They're very good," The Destroyer said in English to

Jenny. "And quite correct. If they're going to oppose our war of liberation, we need to attack and take them out now. It is a pity – I would have thought that they would fight on the side of liberty instead of slavery and oppression."

"Is that my creator?" Saline asked in Japanese, pointing to Akari Soto.

"Yes," The Destroyer said in Japanese.

"She does not look like much of a god," Saline stated. "I will enjoy killing her."

The Destroyer turned to Jenny and smiled. "You are going to meet your creator tomorrow morning. Do with her as you will."

"How long will it take to prepare?" Jenny asked.

"We will be able to attack at dawn," The Destroyer replied.

Jenny nodded. It was a bit of a cliche, but that didn't matter. By tomorrow afternoon she would be holding Alice Matson to account, and every single creator holed up with her would be dead.

Chapter XXVIII – Apotheosis

"We've all grown beyond our stories since we got here."

Atria sat in Volandpanzer's cockpit in front of the Eastern Army Headquarters building, enjoying the morning air through the open upper hatch as they waited for The Destroyer to arrive at the outer perimeter. Near where the mech was standing, Captain Infinite stretched his shoulders, back in his silver tights and black cape. To the other side of the mech, Daiki Yamato crouched, sword in hand. The first task would be to dispose of the orb. Once that was done, they needed to capture or kill The Destroyer and his followers. If all else failed, they would be the second-last line of defence, just ahead of the soldiers inside the building.

Stella and the creators were with Colonel Sato in a command and control centre in the Eastern Army Headquarters building. As Sato said, it was the safest place to them to be. Well, at least, that is what he had written in a note.

In the end, all of their strategic planning had been done with traded notes. With The Destroyer able to watch and listen in on anything they said and did, it was the closest they could get to operational security. Atria didn't like it, but nobody had come up with a better idea. Still, the principles of a defence-in-depth were the same no matter what the intelligence picture. At each intersection leading to the headquarters building were tanks and dug-in infantry, with space for her or Cap to land behind each position and provide support. Cap had set it up well.

"So," she said over the radio. "Your real name's Matthew Markham?"

"That's right," Cap stated. "At least, that's the name I was given when my parents found me. I don't have any memory of who I was before falling out of my home dimension. Once I stopped working at the paper, and all I was doing was being a superhero, there didn't seem to be any need to use it anymore. But, I was always Matthew Markham as well as Captain Infinite – it just took meeting all of you to make me realize that. So, please, just call me Matt."

Atria smiled. She remembered passing Cap...Matt...and Alice sharing a tender moment in the hallway as they prepared to take their positions.

"Matt," Alice was saying. "That's going to take some getting used to."

"I know," Cap had replied. "But, Captain Infinite is a *nom de plume*, a title and a job, not a name. I think I'm ready to be Matt Markham again."

"I feel a bit outclassed here," Daiki said to Atria in Japanese. "Matt can fly and shoot lasers out of his eyes, you've got a battle mech, and I've got a magic sword."

"With luck you won't need to use it," Atria said.

"Speaking of such things," Cap began, "in the interests of full disclosure, after the war I made a promise to myself that I wouldn't take any more lives. Since there's just three or four of them, I'm going to try to keep that promise. I'll be aiming to disable and capture, not kill."

"I understand," Atria said. "Just remember that I'm a soldier, so if I have a kill shot on an active combatant, I will take it."

"Understood," Cap said.

"We have them approaching the outer perimeter on the southeast side," Colonel Sato's voice said over the radio. "Estimated time to contact, fifteen minutes."

Atria pulled the hatch closed and flipped the switches to turn on Volandpanzer's antigrav. "Matt, we're up. This is Silversword, commencing overwatch." Together, she and Cap rose into the air to an altitude of three hundred feet. "I have three targets on the ground, one male, two female."

"This is command," Sato said. "We confirm three targets. You are cleared to engage at will."

"Colonel Sato," Atria said. "You once asked me what I thought of your tanks. I'm afraid I gave you a less-than-honest answer." She grinned and flipped on the targeting. "I think they're *cute*."

And then she fired her first volley of missiles.

Jenny took a deep breath as they walked down the street towards the headquarters building. Beside her, The Destroyer strode with purpose, the orb floating behind him. Behind them, Saline walked so quietly that even with her enhanced senses, Jenny could barely hear her.

"It has begun," the Destroyer said, pointing to two dots rising into the sky. White streaks shot out from one, rocketing towards them, each streak dividing into four.

And then the world exploded around her.

Jenny covered her ears and screamed. The magical barrier kept out the shrapnel and the worst of the shock wave, but not the deafening noise. She opened her eyes and looked around in shock. The Destroyer stood unmoved, his expression placid. But the ground underneath them was gone – they hovered in the centre of a crater at least fifteen feet deep. The faces of the buildings around them had been reduced to rubble by the blast.

And then the second, third, and fourth volleys arrived.

"Volleys are off," Atria said into the radio. "Resuming overwatch."

Atria took a deep breath, reminding herself of the plan. Stage one: attack The Destroyer's shield and force him to drain his power using it. Stage two: separate him and the orb from his followers. Stage three: separate him from the orb and destroy it.

The three targets began to move forward on her scanner, right into the range of the first defensive line. It was time to start working on step two.

"This is Silversword," Atria said. "Targets are within firing range of line 1. Commence bombardment."

Even through the inches of Volandpanzer's armour, she could hear the din of the JSDF tanks beginning to fire.

Jenny was getting used to the noise as the tank shells exploded around her. The barrier around them sparkled with light as the shrapnel ricocheted off it.

"I will deal with the war machines," The Destroyer stated in both English and Japanese without raising his voice. Somehow, despite the noise, she heard him perfectly. "You deal with the survivors."

The Destroyer raised his hand. In the distance Jenny saw dozens of tanks rise into the air, lifted by an invisible force. As they reached a height of a hundred feet, the force rotated them until they were upside down. And then they crashed to the ground. From the corner of her eye, she saw the mech that had been firing missiles plummet to the earth alongside them.

Explosions rippled along the line as some of the tanks exploded, sending the men around them scrambling in disarray. Screams and acrid smoke filled the air.

"There are no war machines left between us and the creators," The Destroyer stated in English and Japanese, waving his hand again. "Accept my protection and deal with the rest."

Jenny felt a pulse of energy surge through her body. Drawing her knives, she dashed towards the first line of men. She was aware of Saline running beside her, almost keeping pace. She heard and felt the gunfire around her, but nothing hit her as she leapt into the defensive line and got stabby.

Warnings screamed at Atria in the cockpit as Volandpanzer crashed to the ground, the shock knocking the wind out of her. Frantically flipping switches, she brought up the internal diagnostics. Autopilot offline – that was no surprise – and she had also lost all of her missile launchers. One of her rapid fire cannons was out of action, as well as the reserve antigrav unit. Servos in the left leg were also damaged – not catastrophic, but it would slow her down.

Pain shot up and down her right leg. She ignored it.

Other than that, she was still fighting fit. She hit the antigrav and brought Volandpanzer back into the air, checking the sensors. "This is Silversword on overwatch," she reported. "We have lost the ground based armour across all lines of defense. It's up to the infantry now. Targets have separated – repeat, targets have separated. Matt, you ready?"

"I'm good to go," she heard Cap say over the radio.

"We are starting stage three," she said, training her remaining rapid fire cannon on The Destroyer and manoeuvring to get closer. She pulled the trigger, sending a stream of tracer rounds on target. The high explosive rounds exploded against his shield. The minute she ceased fire, Cap slammed into the Destroyer, driving them both several blocks away. Atria nodded – everything according to plan. Cap would keep hitting him until he was too far away to interfere, and then use his superior speed to return to help dispose of the orb. And then she saw the warning indicator.

The radiation levels from the orb were spiking.

A cold sweat ran down Atria's back as she landed Volandpanzer beside the orb. It was now glowing red hot. This could only mean one thing.

The containment had reached critical failure. There were only minutes left before detonation. There was no time left to wait for Cap, and even if she did, the radiation was orders of magnitude higher than it had been – Cap wouldn't be able to throw it far enough anyway.

She swallowed. "This is Silversword," she said into the radio. "Power source has reached critical failure and is building up to detonation. I'm going to deal with it." She grabbed the orb with one of the hands of her mech. The orange-hot power orb fused to it. She reached for the afterburners.

"I'm afraid I've got no autopilot," Atria said. "It was an honour to know and serve with all of you."

In the control room, Alice glanced around the room as they heard Atria report. Kaguyama gripped a table, while Stella slumped into her chair and began to weep.

Atria was about to hit the trigger for the afterburners when she heard the upper hatch open behind her.

"I don't think so," Cap said, already pale and sweating from the radiation exposure. "Show me where the controls and the throttle are. I'll take it."

"No!" Atria cried. "You can't! This is from my world – my responsibility! This is from *my* story!"

Cap placed his hand on Atria's shoulder. "We've all grown beyond our stories since we got here," he said. "And you have a promise to keep to Kaguyama."

Atria opened her mouth to protest, but nothing came out. She glanced at the orb – it was glowing orange from the heat. She climbed out and pointed as Cap climbed in. "Steering, throttle, afterburner."

Cap nodded and looked back at her as she jumped to the ground, wincing in pain as she landed, and limped back. "I wish I had somebody who needed me like Kaguyama needs you," he said, and then, with a roar of the afterburners, he and Volandpanzer rocketed into the air and out to sea.

Cap fought back wave after wave of nausea and held the throttle and control stick as steady as he could.

"Matt, what are you doing?" he heard Alice shout over the radio.

"I'm getting the orb to safe distance before it explodes," Cap said. "And making certain an important promise gets kept."

"But you'll die!" Alice cried. "Look, there's got to be

some other way – jump out at the last minute, something!"

"I'm afraid not," Cap said. "Truth be told, this radiation is already doing a number on me. I've barely got enough strength left to control the stick."

"But Matt–"

Cap smiled. "Alice, it's okay. Really, it's okay. Just today, I get to be just like all of you – I get to be mortal. I'm–"

With a blinding flash, the orb detonated, and he was gone.

In the control centre, Alice collapsed to the floor, sobbing.

Chapter XXIX – Reckoning

"The stories I had to tell...that was the price of telling your story."

Daiki Yamato gripped his sword and took a deep breath. He was the second-last line of defence...but what was he supposed to do against this? The line of tanks in front of him had lifted into the air and crashed to the ground upside down, the impact alone almost certainly killing the men inside before overturned tanks scattered throughout the line started exploding. And then there was the flash of the light to the south, and the shock wave. And the radio chatter.

And the firing was getting closer. As were the screams.

"If anybody can hear me, I'm injured, but I'm making my way back on foot," he heard Atria say over the radio, the signal faint. "Captain Markham and Volandpanzer are gone. I'm about five minutes from the outer perimeter. I don't think The Destroyer is far behind."

There was a flurry of gunfire and motion in front of him, and then nothing but moans and screams. His blood went cold when he heard the voice.

"I like to call this game 'arterial spray'," Saline said, picking through the survivors. "Whose will be the highest?"

He saw a flash of movement out of the corner of his eye and dodged, a knife blade tearing through the leather armour and slicing through his arm.

"That wasn't very high!" he heard Saline lament. "Let's see what you can do."

He brought his sword up into a guard position. The American teenager Atria had told him was named Jenny Calhoun looked at him and grinned, a predatory gleam in her eyes and blood trickling down her knives.

She said something in English he didn't understand, and then attacked again. Her knives flashed, his sword striking out to meet them, just a fraction too slow. No killing blow came. Instead she was gone, running into the complex.

"One of them got past me," Daiki reported. "I think it's the—"

An invisible force slammed him against the wall, pinning him in place. He turned his head to see Saline approaching, licking the blood off her knife.

"I finished my game!" she declared with a grin. "I think one of them managed to break three feet!"

"Saline," Daiki gasped. "You need to listen to me. It's—"

"This world is amazing, isn't it?" Saline said. "Back in our world, I had to hide so much of who I am. I had to seem all prim and proper for the royal court, look like a good party member to the other heroes, and I almost never got to have any fun. But here, I'm part of an army of liberation. Here I can kill whoever I want, and be the hero while I do it!"

"You're not a hero," Daiki snarled. "You're just a psychopath showing her true colours!"

"You wouldn't believe all the fantasies I have about you," Saline said, dancing around him. "All the things that half-wolf mongrel 'shield' of yours prevented me from doing. But she's not here, and we are!" She grinned. "And I have hours."

Then, as he struggled against the magic pinning him to the wall to no avail, Saline pulled off his leather armour breastplate and began to slice into his flesh.

"Matt," Alice sobbed. She was aware of Stella and the others looking at her with concern, but ignored them. She used the wall to pull herself to her feet.

"Why didn't I just talk to him?" she heard Mark Gable mutter. "All he wanted me to do was talk to him. Why didn't I do that?"

She looked around the room. On a nearby CCTV feed, she saw Daiki Yamato crouch into a fighting stance.

Air. She needed some air. She stagged out of the room.

"Alice, no, it's not safe!" she heard Stella call out, but kept walking.

How long she walked the corridors she wasn't sure. At some point she heard gunfire, and then silence. She sat down on the floor, staring at the wall.

A convention pamphlet dangled in front of her face. Alice blinked and looked at it. It was a picture of her, labeled in both Japanese and English.

"Hello Alice," she heard a familiar voice say. "I'm Jenny Calhoun." Then the blow fell, knocking her to the floor.

"So, we're going to have a little talk," Jenny said,

picking her up with one hand and throwing her through a door hard enough to break it open. Her side exploded in pain, every breath an agony. As Alice crawled to the corner to get away, she saw Jenny enter the room after her. "And then I'm going to get a bit stabby. I hope that's okay with you." She drew her knife.

"Please," Alice whimpered.

Jenny knelt down close enough that Alice could see that the blood on the knife was still damp. "I just want to know one thing. Why do you hate me?"

Alice blinked. "What? I don't...I don't hate you."

"You really going to lie to me now, creator?" Jenny snarled.

"I love you," Alice said. "I don't hate you at all. I love you to bits. I loved creating you, and writing every moment of you, and seeing you pick yourself up every time you got knocked down. I never, ever hated you."

Jenny looked stunned. Shaking her head, she pointed her knife at Alice's throat. "Then why did you kill everybody I care about? Why is my home overrun with monsters? How can you do that to somebody you love?"

Alice winced as her side throbbed in pain. "Because that what I needed to do to keep telling your story. You're from a network television show. Every season has to have bigger stakes, be more scary, more exciting...and if it isn't, and your numbers slip, they cancel it. And if your show got cancelled, I wouldn't be able to keep you in my life anymore. The stories I had to tell...that was the price of telling your story. And I never ended on a cliffhanger. I always gave you a happy ending, every season. What else could I do for a character I loved?"

The hand holding the knife began to shake.

"When I found out that you were real, and here in the real world, I was so desperate to find you," Alice said, starting to cry. "I wanted to tell you that I was sorry. If I had known that you would be this real, I wouldn't have done...I wouldn't have...I wouldn't have done any of it. I would have given you a different story...I would have..."

Alice hung her head. "I'm sorry."

She heard Jenny slump against the wall, sliding down. When she looked up she saw Jenny staring at her with tears running down her cheeks. And then Jenny pulled out a gun.

Alice closed her eyes tight, waiting for the end. Instead, she felt the grip of the gun pressed into her palm. When she opened her eyes, Jenny was gone.

Alice heard footsteps approaching at a run. Akari Soto appeared at the door. "Alice," she said in English with a heavy accent. "I found you! Jenny Calhoun is in the building, and Saline..." Her voice trailed off as her gaze fell down to the gun in Alice's hand.

Akari knelt down and took the gun. "I'm sorry," she said. "I need this. I'll let the others know you're here." She dashed out of the room.

Alice began to weep.

Daiki screamed in pain as Saline sliced into his flesh again. His left side was a bloody mass. No matter what he did, he couldn't move.

"Don't worry," Saline said. "I'll move to your right side soon. I believe in symmetry."

Then he heard the gunshots. Saline jerked, the knife falling from her hand, and then crumpled. The magic that had pinned him to the wall vanished. He slid down to the ground.

"I'm sorry," he heard Akari Soto say as she rushed towards him, a pistol in her hand. She stood before him, looking him up and down. "Saline was the only character I ever created who was irredeemable. I couldn't let her kill you."

Daiki could only gasp in pain as he tried to rise.

"Are you okay? Akari asked. "I'll get a–"

A spike of masonry impaled and pinned her to the wall beside him. She quivered and was still.

Daiki looked up to see The Destroyer descending from above.

"Rejoice in your liberation," The Destroyer said.

Daiki shook his head. "You killed...she was going to send me home!"

"She was going to continue your enslavement," The Destroyer stated. "The other enslavers – creators – are in this building. Soon all of their creations will be liberated as well."

Daiki tried to rise. As he did, the door opened and Jenny Calhoun dashed out and embraced The Destroyer.

"Roy, thank god you're okay," she said in English. "We have to stop."

"We have only just begun," The Destroyer said in English. "There are so many of us needing to be liberated."

Daiki winced again as he rose to his feet, wishing he could understand what they were saying.

"Jack was right, Roy, Jack was right," Jenny said, holding him tight. "They're just people, all of them. We've gone too far. I love you, Roy. You saved me in every way that I needed to be saved. Let's just go, you and me. We can disappear into one of the created worlds and live the rest of our lives there."

"The war of liberation must not stop," The Destroyer said.

"Please, Roy," Jenny begged, starting to cry. "Please. We've become the monsters. We need to stop. If you don't stop, I'll have to stop you. Please, just stop and come with me."

Daiki gripped his sword with two hands. Pain shot up and down along his side.

"I cannot stop, Jenny," The Destroyer said sadly. "Go if you must."

Jenny drew her knife and swung, stopping at the last minute, the tip resting on The Destroyer's chest. "Please, don't make me," she sobbed. "I'm sorry. I wish I had never talked you into meeting your creator."

The Destroyer put a gentle hand on her head. "I wish you had never lifted your hand against me." Then he threw her against the corner of the opposite building. Daiki heard a loud crack as her spine broke.

Daiki lifted his sword, shaking his head to clear it. The note – the note Akari had passed to him. That was all that mattered now.

"You would still fight?" The Destroyer said in Japanese. "Do you care for your liberation so little?"

"You need to be stopped," Daiki said, his voice almost a whisper.

"You can barely stand," The Destroyer stated. "All the efforts of your friends and army could do little more than slow me down. And you would still fight."

Daiki gripped his sword, struggling to keep the tip on point. The note. He had to remember the note.

"A dear friend of mine believed more than anything that fights should be fair," The Destroyer said. "There is no way this fight can be fair. But, it is not mine to tell you what to do once you are liberated. If you wish to die fighting me, I will respect your wishes. And I will honour the memory of Jack Death. I will let you have the first strike. That at least, will be fair." The Destroyer spread out his arms, thrusting out his chest. "Take your shot."

It was as much of a stagger as it was a thrust. The Black Sword slid into The Destroyer's chest, half of the blade sinking in and piercing his heart. The Destroyer fell to his knees, his eyes wide in shock. Light-headed, Diaki followed him down.

"How?" The Destroyer asked.

"You were a copy of the devil king from my world," Daiki said. "My sword could kill you. My creator – *our* creator – told me so in a note."

The Destroyer looked over to the body of Akari Soto. "She was my real creator?"

Daiki nodded.

"Did...did I have a name?"

"Yes," Daiki said.

"What was my name?"

Daiki shook his head. "I'm sorry, I don't know."

The Destroyer's eyes were dim. "She cared," he whispered, and then was silent.

With what little was left of his strength, Daiki pulled the sword from The Destroyer's body and sat against the wall. He heard irregular footfalls approaching. Looking up, he saw Atria Silversword limping in his direction.

"Are you okay?" she said in Japanese, glancing quickly at him and the bodies of Saline and The Destroyer. "That's a lot of blood." She pressed the transmit button on her radio. "This is Silversword. All targets are down, but we need medics outside behind the final perimeter."

Daiki pointed at where Jenny Calhoun lay still. "I think she may still be alive."

"Then she's one of the few," Atria said.

"This is Sato," a voice called over the radio. "Medics are on the way. Is the perimeter secured?"

"Yes," Atria said. "Everything is secured."

Chapter XXX – Aftermath

"I think it's time to go home and make my story my own."

Atria and Stella stood by the crater at the edge of the perimeter. Construction equipment had begun to arrive, men picking their way around the rubble. A day after the battle, the smoke from burning tanks still hung in the air, but the bodies of the dead had been removed.

"If Cap...I mean, Matt were here, he'd be chiding me right now," Atria said in English, leaning on a cane.

"Why?"

Atria smiled sadly. "I'm making somebody else replace my divot. It's a golf thing. He liked golf."

"Do we have the casualty figures yet?" Stella asked.

"Over six hundred dead," Atria said. She started limping back, Stella following. "According to Jenny Calhoun, Jack Death was killed the day before the attack on Samurai Filmworks. They're looking for his body now, but nothing yet. About all Calhoun can tell us about where they were was that it was a warehouse in the industrial side of town."

"Tokyo's a big city," Stella said.

"That it is," Atria said.

"What about Alice and Daiki Yamato?"

"Alice should be out of the hospital in a couple of days," Atria said, wincing. The medics told her that she had sprained her leg when Volandpanzer crashed, and the swelling was getting bad again. "Same with Daiki. He lost a lot of blood, but he apparently heals very fast. Maybe it's that magic sword of his."

"And what about you?"

"I've had worse."

"I'm not just talking about that."

Atria stopped. "You mean, am I going back when he opens the portal?"

Stella nodded.

"I don't know," Atria said. "I just don't know."

Alice took a deep breath in her hospital bed. The broken rib hurt less now, which was something. The nightmares were a different matter.

She could never unsee what she had seen. Mitsubi weeping beside the body of Akari Soto, which had been pinned to the wall with a spike of masonry. Blood spatters several feet long on the pavement. And then there was Jenny Calhoun, her back bent at an unnatural angle around the corner of a building.

She took a more shallow breath. The painkiller was kicking in.

Mark Gable was probably gone by now. The last she had seen him was while she was being taken out on a stretcher. The only thing she had said as she passed by was, "Matt deserved better than you."

He hadn't answered. Just the thought of Matt – the man known for decades as Captain Infinite – made her want to start crying all over again.

Alice sat up in her hospital bed as Colonel Sato entered. "Forgive my English," he said in a heavy accent, "but we need to talk about Jenny Calhoun."

Alice nodded.

"She was involved in two incidents that the Ministry has classified as terrorist attacks," Sato said. "That is what the public is being told. Under normal circumstances, she would be arrested and handed over to the criminal justice system for trial."

Alice sighed. "How many people did she kill?"

"At this point, the estimate is over a hundred and fifty," Sato replied. "Normally, this would carry the death penalty."

"But these are not normal circumstances," Alice said.

Sato nodded. "That is correct. There is no court in this country that would believe the evidence if we attempted to bring this to trial. Even if there was, there is no precedent for fictional characters coming to life and waging a war against their creators. The Ministry and Japanese Self-Defence Force are both in agreement in this matter – the legal and administrative problems that this situation would create is not desirable."

"So you're not putting her on trial," Alice said.

"That is correct," Sato said. "We are working with the American government to issue her the documentation she will require to return to the United States and deporting her. I understand that she has been permanently paralyzed from the waist down."

"That's what I heard," Alice stated.

"That will have to be punishment enough. Will you take responsibility for your creation?"

Alice nodded. "Of course I will."

"Good," Sato said. "As soon as she is able to travel, you are to take her back with you to the United States, and she will never be permitted to return to this country."

Four days after the battle and one day after the funeral, during which Alice, just out of the hospital, had received condolence after condolence for her loss and Atria had told Stella that she had decided to stay, the barracks where they had once been confined and later lived seemed empty. Stella walked around, looking to see if there was anything she and Adam had left behind. It was their last day there.

Cap's belongings had been removed, as had Akari Soto's. Mark Gable had returned to the United States, and Alice Matson's belongings were now back at her hotel room, where she was resting and waiting for Jenny Calhoun's discharge from the hospital. Then she would be leaving, taking Jenny with her. Kaguyama and Mitsubi had returned to their homes as well.

That just left her, Adam, and Atria. They had a lot to thank Ichiro Takahashi and Worldsoft Games for – Worldsoft had arranged an apartment in Tokyo for her and Adam to use while he recovered once he got out of the hospital. Atria would be joining them to help Stella take care of Adam for a couple of weeks while she figured out what to do next. Stella wasn't sure how they would pay for it, but Takahashi had told her it wouldn't be a problem.

And that just left finishing their packing and moving in.

She heard Atria clear her throat from the door.

"Daiki's about to open the portal," she said, her uniform jacket open to reveal the blouse underneath. "He and Colonel Sato are waiting for us."

Stella nodded. There was nothing they had left behind

anyway. She joined Atria and left the empty barracks behind.

"You asked me a question, back when we first met," Sato said to her in Japanese. "You wanted to know how many unidentified cosplayers had died of exposure in the last ten years."

"I remember," Stella said.

"I received the answer yesterday," Sato stated. "It's seventeen. Now that we know this is an issue, we are going to ensure that in the future this number drops to zero. We will help the children of the creators of Japan call this nation their home."

Stella smiled. "On behalf of all of us, thank you."

"There's a place for you in this effort, if you want it," Sato said.

"Thank you, but I have plans of my own," Stella said. "I have marriage, a degree in quantum physics, and a career decoding the secrets of the universe ahead. And I can't wait to get started."

"And what about you, Major Silversword?" Sato said. "General Yoshida wanted you to know that there is place for you in the Japanese Self-Defence Force, at your current rank, if you would like it."

Atria smiled. "As tempting as that is, I think I'm ready to spend some time enjoying civilian life. So, I'll pass, for now."

They turned the corner to find Daiki Yamato waiting for them in the square, his sword in hand and leather armour hidden under his cloak.

Sato bowed to Daiki. "Before you leave, I just wanted to express our gratitude for your assistance during these recent events."

Daiki smiled. "You're very welcome."

Atria nodded. "You saved everybody. You should be proud."

"So, it's just me going back?" Daiki asked.

"I spent the last ten years of my life fighting a war to save my world," Atria said. "Now that I know there's a replacement me back there, I think it's time for my war to end. Besides, I've been talking with Kaguyama, and I'm going to help him finish my story. As Matt said, Kaguyama needs me – and I can do more to make sure my story has a happy ending by staying here than I can if I go back."

"My life has been here in this world for years," Stella said. "This is my home."

Daiki nodded to both of them. "I can respect that."

"What about you?" Stella said. "Your creator is dead. There's nobody to finish your story now. Are you sure you want to go back?"

"Oh yes," Daiki said. "Athena is waiting for me, and she must be very worried. And, besides, now I know I've been living in a story written by somebody else for all these years. I think it's time to go home and make my story my own."

"Good luck!" Atria said.

"Good luck!" Stella said.

"And you," Daiki said, swinging his sword. A glowing portal appeared. He stepped through, and it disappeared behind him.

Atria and Stella stood looking at where Daiki had been standing for a moment. Behind them, Sato made his apologies and left.

"I'm going to the hospital," Stella said. "Meet you back at the apartment?"

"Sure," Atria replied. "I've got to finish cleaning out my office anyway. It turns out that they're happy to issue me the documentation I need to live in this world for free, but if I want to keep using my office, I have to either join the JSDF or pay rent. Go figure."

Stella spent the taxi ride to the hospital in silence. Once she got up to Adam's hospital room, she found him sitting up in his bed, watching anime.

"Well," she said, giving him a kiss, "it's done."

Epilogue – Six Months Later

"Adam Jacobs has a secret: he's going to marry a
character from a video game."

Stella sat with Atria at the coffee table in their Tokyo
apartment. Colour swatches covered the table. Stella still
couldn't believe that in addition to paying for the
apartment while Adam convalesced, WorldSoft Games
had also volunteered to cover the cost of holding their
wedding in Japan.

"You can't keep pushing this off on me," Atria said.
"You need to make your own decision about the colours.
The wedding's only two months away."

"You're the maid of honour," Stella replied. "You
have a say in this too."

"Shouldn't you be discussing this with Adam?" Atria
said. "He's the one you're marrying, after all."

"He's good at analysing colours," Stella stated, "Not
picking them." She leaned back. "So, how are things with

you and Kaguyama?"

Atria stretched her arms and smiled. "The page proofs arrived yesterday. Aiko's illustrations look amazing. But, I think the typesetter might be trolling us. I could swear there are random errors that have been thrown in. I had to send in four pages of corrections."

"Looking forward to flying solo?"

Atria took a deep breath. "Next book is the one, isn't it? Just my words and Kaguyama's outline."

"Scared?"

Atria smiled. "A bit. I never thought I'd be saving my world this way. But, once I'm done with this series, I've got some ideas of my own for something new. Aiko's already agreed to do the illustrations for it."

"Stella," Adam called from the bedroom they had converted into a home office. "You need to see this."

Stella got up and walked into the office. Adam had received an early access copy of WorldSoft Games' *Chronicles of Arcaniana II*, localized into English, and had been playing it on his laptop since yesterday afternoon.

"The note they sent with it said I really needed to check out this one area," he said. "Apparently, it's your parent's manor. I didn't understand the urgency until I saw this." He pointed at the screen.

A drawing of one of her family's servants was on the screen. As she read the dialogue bubble, she had to steady herself on the desk with quivering hands.

"Their highnesses are not available," the servant said. "They've journeyed to another world to attend their daughter's wedding."

There was a knock at the front door. Stella bolted to answer it.

Jenny Calhoun reclined in her wheelchair and basked in

the California sunlight. Behind her, Alice Matson sifted through the mail.

"You've got pamphlets from three colleges for their high school diploma programs," Alice called. "Number three is here. You gonna pick one soon?"

"Do I have to?" Jenny asked.

"You need to have a life of your own," Alice replied. "And I didn't create you to be somebody who could be stopped by as insignificant a thing as a wheelchair."

"I *was* in high school," Jenny said.

"You really want to go back to that after all of this?"

Jenny frowned. "Fair point."

Alice checked her watch. "Ah, Freddie will be here in a couple of minutes. She can't wait to meet you, after all that time she spent playing you in the show."

"Does she have to?" Jenny asked. "This is going to feel really weird."

"Freddie McClaren had a lot of input into how your character developed over the series," Alice said. "In some ways, she's almost as much your creator as I am. Besides, I need her help to plan out the series finale. A proper happy ending, as promised." She paused. "Don't worry – you'll get along fine. I know it."

Somebody knocked at the screen door. The spitting image of Jenny waved, holding a plastic bag in her other hand.

Alice let her in and introduced her. Freddie looked at Jenny and grinned.

"You must be the real deal," she said. "I have just two things to say to you: first, it was my greatest honour and privilege to be able to portray you on the screen. And second," she motioned at the wheelchair, "what the hell happened to you in Japan?"

After Jenny got over her shock, she began to laugh. Alice smiled. "I knew you two would get along. Besides,

232

I think you should be sitting in on this discussion. This is your happy ending we're here to talk about."

Freddie nodded. "Indeed. By, the way, Alice, what's with the old comic book you wanted me to pick up for you? This thing's gotta be seventy or eighty years old – I don't want to think about how much you must have paid for it."

Alice took the bag and pulled out the comic book. On its worn cover a superhero in silver tights and a black cape flew towards the reader, a smile on his face.

"I just wanted to see a dear friend happy again," Alice said, a quiver in her voice.

Junichi Kaguyama sat at his writing desk and flipped through the page proofs of the final book of his career. Atria's writing style was sprinkled throughout, so similar and yet different from his own.

He smiled. He knew that he would never be able to write another book again – he had forgotten too much of the craft. But, his story would be finished anyway by somebody who would care about it more than anyone else ever could.

For the first time since his diagnosis, he felt okay with what would happen next.

There was still one piece of business that needed to be taken care of. It was a gamble – Kaguyama didn't know if she would accept or not, and it required her consent. But he didn't think she'd refuse. He'd surprise her with it the next time he saw her, either here at his home or at the apartment that she shared with Stella and Adam.

With a flourish of his pen, Kaguyama signed the adoption paperwork that would officially make Atria Silversword his daughter.

Mark Gable stared at the screen of his computer with annoyance. His old editor at Superhero Comics was pestering him over email yet again. With a sigh, Mark opened the email to take a look at what the man had to say this time.

"Look, I know you're going through some kind of late mid-life crisis and want to stretch your wings, but I've got a run of *The Human Spider* that needs a lead writer, and none of these new kids knows how to pace a story for shit. I can give you a 5% raise if you come back for Monday, OK?"

Mark rolled his eyes, and then hit reply.

"I told you that I quit," he typed. "Go find somebody else's story pitches to tear up." Then he hit send, and closed the email program.

It was a risk, he knew, but it was worth it. He had reached out to Jake Edwards, an old college friend of his who had ended up as a managing editor at Worldwide Books, shortly after getting back from Japan. The conversation that followed was as much Mark calling in a favour as it was a story pitch.

"Wow, Mark, that's really out of your wheelhouse," Jake said. "You sure you want to do this?"

"Absolutely," Mark said. "Time to get out of this rut I've been stuck in for most of my career."

"Alright," Jake said. "I know what you can do when you're treading water, so I can't wait to see what you can do at your best. I'll get legal to draw up the contract. Just email me the contact info for your agent."

And with that, the deal was done. Five and a half months later, the manuscript was almost finished. A story about the inner lives of his characters – their hardships, triumphs, and failures. The sort of story he had held back from writing for decades because he was afraid that it wouldn't pay the bills. He still didn't know if it would.

The money from the advance was going to run out in two months. But at least it would be something he could be proud of. There was just one last touch to add: the dedication.

He knew exactly who it needed to be dedicated to. He put his fingers on the keyboard.

"To Captain Matthew Markham," he typed.

An hour after my parents had left the apartment for their hotel, my mind was still racing. In a single moment, I had regained everything I thought I'd lost those five years ago when I fell through the world into a cold, wet alleyway.

I never had imagined my parents being as emotional as they were. Then again, my tears had flowed freely as well, particularly when my father gave his blessing to our marriage and filled out my guest list. All of my siblings will be attending, as well as my comrades in the Hero of Prophecy's party. And all of this was because of WorldSoft Games. The spell Ichiro Takahashi built into all of their character descriptions allows them to come and go between worlds as they please, and they all know where I am and what happened to me.

But while they can travel between worlds, I can't. The spell requires magic I'd lost long ago. But that no longer matters – my family and comrades can come to me even if I can't come to them. My father told me how to create the summoning circle that would direct them to wherever I was.

I glanced into our bedroom. Adam was sleeping on his side with a light snore. Atria was off enjoying a girl's night with Mitsubi. I smiled as I thought of everything that had happened since we got to Japan, and everybody we had met. Of Atria, who wanted to save her world and became my best friend, and Captain Infinite, who just wanted somebody to talk to. Of Daiki Yamato, who wanted to go home, and Jenny Calhoun, who wanted to know why her creator had made her suffer. Of Jack Death, who didn't know what compassion was, and The Destroyer, who died without ever knowing his own name but who learned in the end that his real creator had cared after all.

They all deserved to be remembered. But for that to happen, somebody had to tell their story, just like one of their creators would do.

The decision was easy. Atria had kept in touch with the others, so I could get their parts of the story easily enough. I stepped into the home office and sat down. I opened my laptop and turned on the word processor. And then I began to type.

Adam Jacobs has a secret: he's going to marry a character from a video game.

Afterword – Re: *Re:Apotheosis*

In the beginning, there was *Re:Creators*.

Well, that's not quite true. In the beginning, there was *The Last Action Hero*. And, that would be where the story of this particular tale begins.

The Last Action Hero was a 1993 movie starring Arnold Schwarzenegger, Austin O'Brien, and Charles Dance. The first half of the movie involved O'Brien's character Danny Madigan being sucked into Schwarzenegger's latest movie and teaming up with his character, Jack Slater. The second half had Jack Slater and Danny leaving the film-within-a-film and facing off against said film's villain, Benedict (Charles Dance), in the real world.

The first half was a lightweight and very funny send-up of American action movies. The second half was more serious, and by far the more interesting. Both Jack Slater and Benedict have to process the fact that they are fiction, and face a real world that is very different from their own. It also hinted at the potential for an epic story, in which Benedict would bring movie villains out into the real world to cause havoc. Unfortunately, since it was a movie with a limited running time, this never came to pass – Benedict dies right after revealing his plan.

I saw it when I was a teenager, and it made an impression, albeit one that didn't go very far beyond "Neat!" Part of this probably had to do with this other little movie that released at the same time called *Jurassic Park*. But, I think most of was because fictional characters coming into conflict in – and coming to grips with – the real world needed a series rather than a movie. This sort of concept needs space, and an hour of screen time is not even close to enough.

Happily, in Japan *The Last Action Hero* also made an impression on Rei Hiroe, author of *Black Lagoon*, and Ei Aoki, the director of *Fate Zero*. The story goes that they decided that they wanted to make an anime version of the concept, and started contacting various rights holders to bring existing characters into the real world to battle it out. The problem was that nobody could agree on whose character would win in a fight. So, they decided to use expies of various character types in Japanese pop culture instead.

The result was *Re:Creators*, a 2017 series produced by Troyca and streamed on Amazon Prime. The series is amazing – I consider it a masterpiece – and epic. To avenge her fallen creator, who was driven to suicide by what we would recognize today as akin to a nascent cancel culture, an overpowered fan character named Altair comes into reality with the intention of making the fictional worlds collide with the real one, destroying them all in the process. The characters she brings into the real world divide into two sides, with a JRPG NPC character named Meteora Österreich, alongside a mech-piloting magical knight named Selesia Upitiria, leading the side trying to save reality, while Altair's side crystallizes around Aliceteria February, a magical knight from a grimdark world, and Mamika Kirameki, a magic girl from a children's show. Both sides are joined by other characters from a variety of Japanese media genres.

What elevated the show beyond a goofy genre-crossing team-up was these characters' interactions with their creators. Each character underwent an existential crisis upon realizing that they were fiction, and being in the same world as their creators allowed some truly amazing story and emotional beats to take place. I'm not going to spoil it – *Re:Creators* is a must-see if you like this sort of thing – but the end result was a deep dive into how we create, why we create, and how we relate to what we create.

I discovered the show while recovering from surgery in the early days of the pandemic. I was new to anime (a friend of mine, Chris Willmore, had tried to introduce me properly to it in the late 1990s by showing me episodes of *Ramna ½*, but it hadn't stuck), and *Re:Creators* blew me away. It got under my skin in a way that almost nothing else had, to the point that I avoided doing a rewatch for almost two years because I didn't want to see certain beloved characters die again. But I did do a rewatch around the end of 2021, and something happened: a sequel series began writing itself in my head.

To put it mildly, this was a problem.

I have been at a professional level of non-fiction writing since 1998, and a professional level of fiction writing since *Diablo Demonsbane* in 2000. I've owned my own publishing company since 2007. When you reach this level of professional competency, there are certain things you are no longer able to do – writing fanfiction is among them.

So, my brain was coming up with scenes for a story that I wouldn't be able to tell without permission from the rights holders. Who happened to be in Japan. And did I mention that I can't speak or write Japanese?

I don't remember quite how long it took me to make the decision, but in the end I decided, "What the hell, why not?" J. Michael Straczynski, the creator of *Babylon 5*, had once pitched a reboot of *Star Trek* to Paramount. So, I would take a page out of his book, and pitch a sequel series to Troyca. In this pitch I would explain my approach and make an argument for it being the correct one to do justice to the material, and then lay out the plot that was writing itself in my head. As I started working on the pitch, I also began researching what the procedure would be for an English-speaking Canadian to pitch a series to a Japanese anime studio.

The answer, as it turns out, was "he doesn't." It wasn't that much of a surprise, really. Anime studios are busy, and directors already have a long list of passion projects that they want to make. They're not going to take a pitch from somebody who can't even speak their language of business. Pitching to Troyca was a no-go. But that still left the story writing itself in my head with no signs of stopping.

So, I decided to make it a stealth pitch. I'd frame it as a hypothetical – "This is what I would do if I was writing a *Re:Creators* sequel series" – with a bunch of comments built into the plot outline about why I made certain story decisions where I did. By the time it was done, the stealth pitch was around 40 double-spaced pages long. The returning characters were Meteora, Selesia, Selesia's creators Matsubara and Marine, and Sota (the narrator and protagonist). I posted it in two parts on Medium, put a link up to each part in the *Re:Creators* subreddit, and then told myself that it was done, the story was told in a way that I was actually allowed to tell it, and I could move on.

My brain, stubborn bastard that it can be, didn't listen. Scenes kept writing themselves in my head.

To put it mildly, this was a problem.

The option always existed of writing it as an original story – a spiritual sequel instead of a direct sequel. This presented two challenges. First, all of the returning characters would need to be changed, which was relatively easy. What I was doing with Matsubara and Marine was so different from the original series that all they needed was a name change and a different physical description. Meteora, Selesia, and Sota would need to become new characters with different back stories, but that wasn't hard either. The tough part was the second challenge – I needed a new cosmology, something different enough that it could be its own original universe, but also at least approaching the quality and depth of the cosmology of the original series. That one took my brain over a month.

But then, at the beginning of April, my brain figured it out. Now I just needed to know if anybody would actually want to read the thing (an important question when one is about to embark on a fairly large project while having a mortgage to pay and a family to feed). So, I put the question to the *Re:Creators* subreddit, and the answer came back as a definitive "yes."

The writing felt more like an exorcism than anything else. It poured onto the page. Meteora became Princess Stellaria, aka Stella; Selesia became Atria Silversword; Sota was transformed into Adam Jacobs; and Matsubara and Marine became Kaguyama and Mitsubi. These characters arrived almost fully formed in my head. By the time the serial went live at the end of May on Tapas, the draft of the entire book was finished.

Just as *Re:Creators* was Rei Hiroe's exploration of his media landscape, *Re:Apotheosis* is my exploration of mine – the media I grew up with, that I consumed in the past, and that I am consuming right now. It also includes the stories I have heard of the Western media as an industry, and the many people I have met since I became a published author.

Kaguyama's condition is inspired by Sir Terry Pratchett, who I had the great pleasure and privilege of meeting and having a cup of coffee with at Worldcon in Toronto in 2003. Sir Terry was a wonderful man, as charming and funny in real life as he was in print, and that cup of coffee made my day, despite blanking on any subject to talk about as soon as I sat down. His diagnosis of Early-Onset Alzheimers' was heartbreaking. The possibility of having one's ability to create slowly taken away is the stuff of pure nightmare for any writer. I would like to think that Sir Terry's creations, had they known him, would have forgiven him for not being able to continue their stories just as Atria forgives Kaguyama. It is a pleasant author's fantasy, at any rate.

Atria herself is inspired by the many officers I met and read about while working on my Master of Arts degree in the War Studies program at the Royal Military College of Canada, as well as my work in military history through my little publishing company over the last couple of years. She is an officer and a soldier through and through, and I would like to think that if she was to encounter some of her real world peers, they would recognize one of their own.

Mark Gable is based on a story about the comic book industry from a show in the early 1990s called *Prisoners of Gravity*. *Prisoners of Gravity* was an interview show produced by Mark Askwith and hosted by Rick Green that aired on TV Ontario, with the conceit that Green was trapped in a satellite interviewing people in science fiction and fantasy. One of the episodes was about the rise of independent publishers in the comic book industry, which at the time was fairly well known for burning out creatives. The particular story, as I remember it, was about this artist who wanted to display one of his full-page spreads at an art show. In response, his editor ripped the picture to shreds in front of him and instructed him to redraw it, making the point that the artist had no ownership of his work in the most brutal manner possible.

Jenny Calhoun is an expy of *Buffy the Vampire Slayer*. Western media doesn't really have the magical girl as an archetype in the same way that Japan does, but it does have a type of magical girl, and this was codified by Buffy Summers. Her world is likewise inspired by the show, particularly this odd tendency in Western television to need the stakes to be higher every single season, which doesn't take too long to reach a point of absurdity. In the case of the Buffyverse, by the end of the show the characters were lampshading the number of apocalypses they had personally stopped.

Alice Matson is the closest thing to an author-insert character in the entire story, and her character arc reflects my evolving views of Superman (of whom Captain Infinite is an expy). Her rant about Captain Infinite is almost word-for-word what I have said about Superman, for which I was (quite correctly) criticized for a lack of imagination in the LoadingReadyRun Twitch chat.

The wartime history of Captain Infinite was a late addition to his character (one of the delightful things that happens when a character springs to life is that writing him becomes an act of discovery in and of itself), and inspired by the post-war careers of soldiers from units such as Easy Company in the 101st Airborne (made famous by *Band of Brothers*). When writing the book, Stephen E. Ambrose noticed that the vast majority of these men, who had spent so much time killing during the war, went into careers that were the polar opposite of soldiering, such as teaching or construction. Captain Infinite's version of this is his decision to use his powers to protect people, but to never take another life. I can't say for certain that his unit – the 42nd Rangers – isn't a *Hitchhiker's Guide to the Galaxy Reference*, but if it is, it is an unconscious one.

Jack Death is an expy – well, "rip-off" would be the more accurate term – of John Wick, and a bit of a commentary on the "mockbuster" phenomenon in Western media. Admittedly, I did also take a bit of iconoclastic delight in giving the Mamika role of *Re:Creators* to John Wick (this will make sense if you've seen the show).

Daiki Yamato is an expy of *isekai* protagonists like Naofumi from *Rising of the Shield Hero* and Hajime from *Arifureta*. This genre has become huge in the years since *Re:Creators* aired, and is now a massive part of the anime landscape. Likewise, The Destroyer is inspired in part by the many devil or demon kings who litter the *isekai* genre to the point that they are probably their own sub-trope.

Daiki Yamato's creator, Akari Soto, is inspired by the light novel and anime industries. Light novel series can run for dozens of volumes, and to a Western reader can seem a bit reminiscent of Robert Jordan's *Wheel of Time* series, where the rumour was that he was using the books as a cash cow and just updating his outline for the final volume as each new book was written. The relationship of Japan's anime industry to its literature is very different from Western media – where in Western media a television adaptation is independent from its source material, and as such the relative success of the source material is irrelevant to the perceived success of the adaptation, in Japan many anime adaptations exist to market their source material. This means that one is far more likely to see an anime adaptation of an ongoing series than one is to see an adaptation of a completed one, and the failure to boost light novel or manga sales can doom an otherwise successful anime. All of this, in turn, leads to Akari Soto stringing poor Daiki Yamato along until she can get a series.

Last but not least, The Destroyer's creator, Habiki Matoyami, is a hack. Hack writers exist in the creative industry and probably always will. He does, however, also represent the grimdark philosophy of storytelling, in which reality is depicted as being violent and hopeless, where good characters suffer terrible fates while evil characters flourish. It's not a philosophy of storytelling that I share (and, I would argue, it's a misinterpretation of what George R.R. Martin is actually doing in *A Song of Ice and Fire*, which was limited to removing plot armour from the characters).

And that is the story of *Re:Apotheosis*. I hope you enjoyed reading it as much as I enjoyed creating it.

About the Author

Robert B. Marks is an author, editor, researcher, and publisher. He is the author of *Diablo: Demonsbane*, the e-book that launched the entire Blizzard fiction line back in 2000, as well as *The EverQuest Companion*, the *Garwulf's Corner* pop culture columns, and he is the co-author of *The Eternity Quartet* with Ed Greenwood.

As a non-fiction author and historian he is the co-author of *A Funny Thing Happened on the Way to the Agora: Ancient Greek and Roman Humour*, with R. Drew Griffith, as well as the translator of Grandmaison's *Training of the Infantry for Offensive Combat*, the French doctrine of 1913, and Moltke the Younger's *Memories, Letters and Documents*.

Put another way, he wears many hats. One is a Stetson, and the other a Tilly. He lives in the area of Kingston, Ontario, with his wife and children.